Deadly Ruck

Ruck Boys
Book 6

Maggie Alabaster

Trigger Warnings

Mentions of sexual assault.

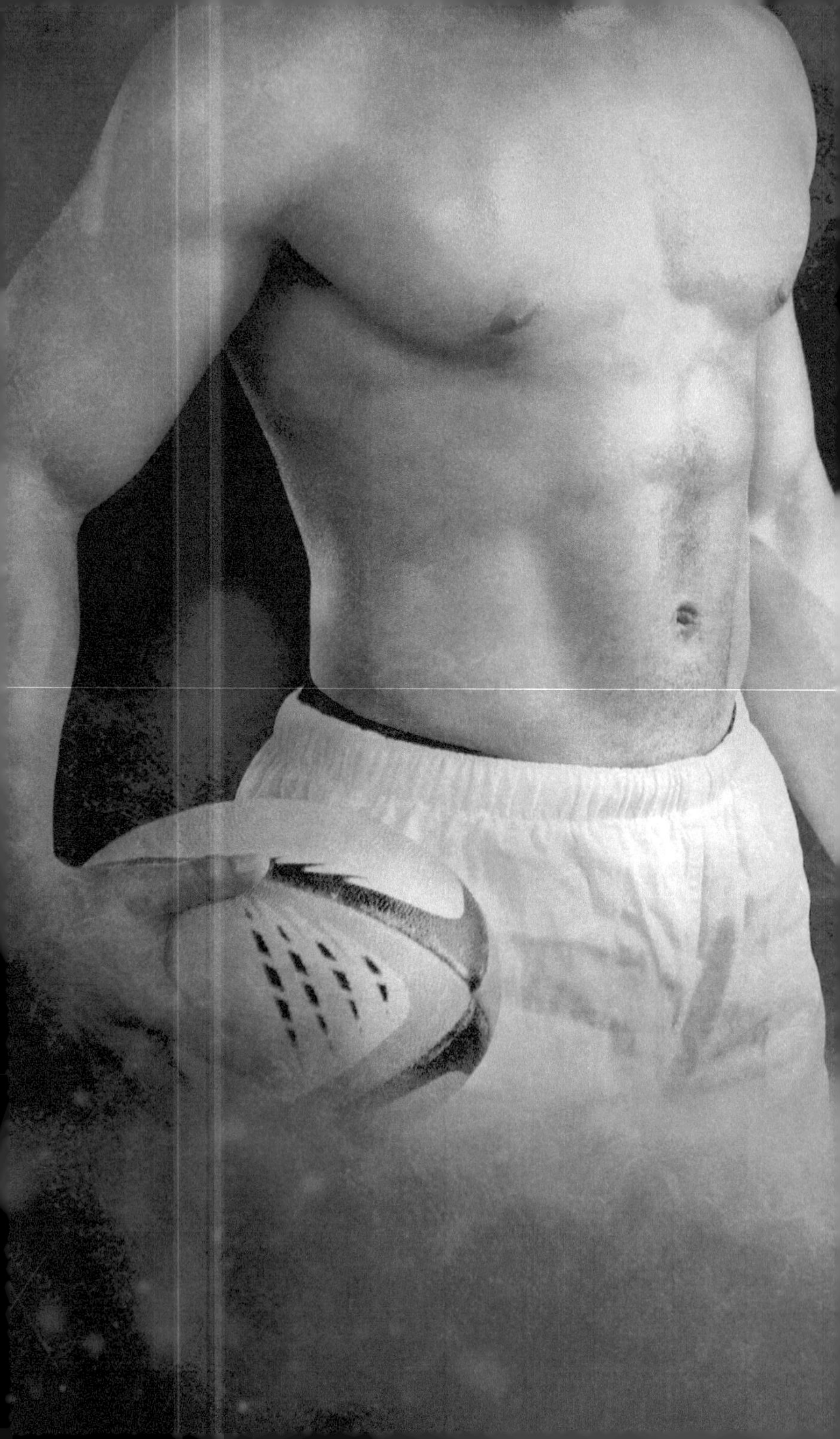

Chapter One

Chelsea

THE DARKNESS WAS ABSOLUTE.

I tried to shake the hood off my face, but it wouldn't budge.

The zip tie which bound my wrists together was too tight for me to slip my hands free. The second the back of the car was shut behind me, I tried. All I did was chafe my skin, rubbing it against the hard plastic until it was all but raw.

I wanted to shout for help, but no one would have heard me over the roar of the engine, and the traffic around us. Traffic that gradually tapered off before the car slowed and turned onto a dirt road.

I managed to suppress blind panic, but fear refused to lessen, much less dissipate.

Terror mixed with disappointment. Scared of who grabbed me and threw me in the back of a car, and the expectation of what they might do to me. Disappointment in myself for letting it happen. I was lost in my head, angry at being fired. I let it distract me. I should have been paying attention, and I wasn't.

I let my guard down and now... I was going to suffer for it.

I was going to die.

Fuck!

I could have screamed at the universe. At the the timing too. How had the press learned about my past? Why did anyone give a shit about what I used to do?

I used to take my clothes off for money, so what? It shouldn't have been anyone's business but mine. It sure as hell shouldn't have been the news headline. Not in Dusk Bay, or anywhere else. If I lived long enough to find out who told them, I was going to make them fucking pay.

All of this, right now, was their fault.

Okay, and mine. I knew this day had to come, and I still wasn't ready for it. Now, here I was, in the back of a car, being taken to fuck knows where. Had my guys noticed I was missing yet? If they hadn't, they would soon enough. They were going to be furious.

They'd burn the world down until they found me.

I couldn't shake the feeling they might already be too late.

Underneath me, the car jolted, bouncing over the rough road. I was thrown against the side of the car, my shoulder hitting the boot door hard.

I cried out from the sudden pain. Nothing was broken, but that was going to bruise. Tears prickled my eyes.

Don't lose your shit, I told myself. *The only way you get out of here in one piece is if you keep it together. You're Chelsea fucking Miller. Doctor Chelsea fucking Miller. You're smart, strong and resourceful. If you let them freak you out, they have the upper hand.*

I wanted to tell my inner voice they already had the upper hand, but she was right. I had to remain calm. If I didn't, I'd miss potential opportunities to save my own ass. All I needed was one. A turn back. A window I could push open. Something. Rational thought and patience would find a chance for me. Not freaking out.

I focused on my breathing. In and out, slowly. Visualised arriving home, the guys all hugging me. All of them having worried about me. Laughing it off as though this was nothing.

The car slowed and came to a stop.

This is it, I told myself. *Whatever happens now, you'll be fine. You've been through stuff before, you'll get through this.*

The engine died and the car doors opened and thudded shut. Footsteps crunched on gravel, around to the back of the car. The boot was opened, bringing with it a rush of cooler air.

Hands slid under my body, lifting me before I was thrown over a shoulder. Blood rushed to my head. Once again, I forced myself to keep calm. Keep breathing. Keep listening and thinking and paying attention.

Judging by the sound of footsteps around us, we weren't alone. I couldn't tell how many of them there were. A few at least. People who worked for Dominic King, Nyla Fox and Carlos Jones.

What did they want from me?

Carlos Jones and the Crimson Viper cartel dealt in human trafficking. I couldn't rule out that was their intention here. They'd sell me to someone who wanted to use my body until he was tired of me.

I swallowed back a knot of panic that tried to work its way back up. If that was what they had planned for me, I'd deal with it. I'd find a way to escape and get back at them, twice as hard. Whatever happened, I'd be a survivor.

Keys jangled and a door was unlocked. Whoever carried me walked up several wooden steps and across a wooden floor.

The door was closed behind us and locked with an ominous couple of clicks.

I was carried deeper into the structure and lowered down. I found something soft under me. A mattress.

I couldn't help the shiver of fear that passed through me. I was right. They'd brought me here to rape me. If I had to guess, I'd bet we were a long way from anything or anyone. If I screamed, no one would hear. Should I try anyway?

No, I had to keep myself contained. Pretend I wasn't scared out of my wits.

The mattress dipped as a heavy body lay down beside me and placed a hand on my hip. Reflexively, I flinched. Tried to roll away. They grabbed me and pulled me back.

"Where do you think you're going?" A male voice growled.

I froze.

What the fuck?

"What the fuck? Storm?"

The hood was yanked up over my head, messing my hair. I looked over into his amused, stormy grey eyes.

"Who else? No one is allowed to kidnap you but us." He jerked his head to the other five guys, who sat or stood beside the mattress.

I struggled to sit up, my hands still bound behind my back. "You scared the shit out of me. I thought you were—" I blinked back ridiculous tears. Why was I crying right now?

Frost and Dallas came to sit on either side and wind their arms around me.

"We didn't mean to scare you," Frost said. "We saw your text message about being fired and figured you'd want some help taking your mind off that. The last time we did this, you liked it." He looked full of regret, eyes sad, mouth turned down.

"We're sorry," Dallas whispered.

"I'm not," Storm said. "You should have known we wouldn't let anyone do this to you. If they had—"

"You would have rearranged their face," Atlas and Jay finished his sentence for him simultaneously.

"Fucking right I would." He gave them a nod.

"You want to take this off?" I jerked my head over my shoulder, in the direction of the zip tie.

It was Ramsey who hurried to the kitchen to search for something sharp. He came back with a knife, which he used to carefully slice through the plastic, freeing my wrists.

I shook them out and rubbed them for a while. "I don't know if I should be angry at you guys or touched. Most guys wouldn't think to kidnap their girlfriend to cheer her up. That's really sweet."

Storm was right, I should have known they wouldn't let it happen.

"Definitely touched," Frost said.

"Touched is perfect," Dallas agreed. He placed the tips of his fingers on my chin and turned my face to kiss me. "That's what we brought you here for."

"All the touching." Frost turned my head so he could kiss me too.

The team was going to notice the absence of half of its players, but I couldn't bring myself to care right now. If I ever needed to let off steam and be loved, it was now. Right here. Now I appreciated the fact I could scream and not be overheard.

Between them, Dallas and Frost eased my clothes off until I was naked on the mattress in front of all of my guys.

"Now she's here, we should keep her that way," Atlas said, picking up items of my clothing and tucking them under his arm.

"I like how you think," Jay said. "She looks perfect like that."

"Maybe we should," Storm agreed. "We could stay here forever. Order in food once in a while."

"Too many people would miss you," I said as Frost slowly made his way down my body with his mouth, kissing here and sucking there before lowering his head between my legs, tasting my pussy with his tongue.

"I could retire," Storm said stubbornly. He shook his head to himself and started to shed his clothes.

In a minute or two, I was surrounded by six, naked muscular men who all loved me. The lingering fear of the last couple of hours was gone from my mind. The only thing that mattered right now was skin on skin and Frost's tongue on my clit.

Dallas lavished attention on my breasts with his mouth, sucking one nipple, then the other. Every couple of minutes, he switched to the opposite one, making certain they both got their fair share of spoiling.

"Why do you always taste so good?" Frost asked. He smiled at me with his eyes while tracing circles around my clit piercing with the tip of his tongue.

"I could ask you the same question," I said, my breath already ragged. There was nothing about any of them that didn't feel and taste good.

"Pineapple," Ramsey said simply.

I choked back a laugh, which ended abruptly when Frost pressed a couple of fingers inside me, hooking them around and rubbing them over my G spot.

"You're weird," Storm told him.

"Thank you," Ramsey said graciously. He stood watching Frost while slowly stroking his hand up and down his erection.

"Make her come," Storm said to Frost.

Frost made a noise of agreement in the back of his throat and worked me more firmly with his tongue and fingers.

Who was I to argue? I arched my back and shouted to the ceiling as the first orgasm claimed me. I was barely down when Frost was kneeling between my knees and sliding his cock into me.

"Mmm." I exhaled slowly as he slid in and out of me, our bodies making wet sucking sounds with each thrust. His bare skin slapped against mine over and over, the sound mesmerising.

"Come inside her," Storm told him. "We all want to watch."

"Yes, we do," Ramsey agreed.

Atlas groaned. "I find myself agreeing with Storm again."

Storm chuckled. "When you're right, you're right."

"It had to happen eventually," Atlas teased.

"Fuck off," Storm told him, but it was a brotherly tone, not the antagonistic one they used to share.

"Ignore them," Frost said as he drove into me. "I'm trying to."

"Ignore who?" I joked, my eyes half-closed. "I can't hear anything. Just us fucking."

"That's all that matters," he said. He grunted and thrust frantically before crying out and coming deep inside me. "So... good. So... fucking good." He fell still, filling me with his cum, before finally sagging and rolling off me.

Before anyone else could move, Dallas left my breasts and shuffled over between my legs. He lifted them to drape them over his shoulders before slamming hard inside me. His eyes wild, he thrust desperately, no more than a handful of times before it was his turn to come, filling me further.

"So fucking incredible," he whispered. He panted

and clung to me for a minute or two before lowering my legs and reluctantly rolling away.

On some unseen signal, Storm was beside me, rolling me over and pulling me to my hands and knees. He knelt behind me, gripped my hips and positioned his cock outside my pussy. Slowly, he eased inside me until he was seated all the way in.

"You're so warm and wet," he marvelled. "So damn perfect."

I must have been very wet from the cum of two men inside me, but that didn't deter him at all. He pulled me back onto him with one hand while reaching around with the other to pinch my nipple. I cried out, but it felt so good. Even better when he did it again, and again.

"You're going to make me come again," I said.

"Good," he said gruffly. "Come again." He pressed his hand between us to rub his thumb over my clit while he slowed down his thrusts.

"What are you going to do if I don't?" I asked.

His response was to pinch my clit so hard I came then and there. Intense and long. I forgot the world existed for a minute or two.

Storm swore as my muscles contracted around his cock, making him come too. "Fucking hell, woman," he growled. "You're something else. So fucking something else." He grunted a couple of times, thrusting slowly until he was done. He slid out of me and rolled me over into my back.

"It's about time," Atlas said, all but shoving him out of the way and hovering over me. He rolled me onto my side and lay behind me. Bending my knees to spread my legs, he inched his cock inside me. "I thought I was going to explode if I didn't fuck you soon."

"That was the idea," Storm said. "To see how long it'd be before you exploded."

"Don't make a mess in my cabin," Frost said. "Except this kind of mess. This is fine. We don't need bits of Atlas all over the cabin."

"Lucky Storm finished so fast then," Atlas said. He stroked a hand up and down my side as he slid out of me and back in again.

"I did not finish that fast," Storm protested.

Atlas chuckled, his breath warm on my shoulder.

"You guys," I said with a laugh.

They were quiet then while Atlas fucked me, slowly, then fast, then slowly again. Until he couldn't hold back and came inside me too. He grunted and moaned, thrusting faster still until his body stilled except for a quiver of orgasm. Finally, he flopped down, holding me close for a few minutes before pulling away and letting Jay take his place.

Jay lay down on his back, pulling me over him, sliding me down onto his erection. His eyes on mine, he gripped my waist and guided me up and down, my breasts bouncing as I rode him. With each bounce, my clit rubbed against his belly, pushing me into a third orgasm, then a fourth.

With the fourth, Jay came too, his fingers digging into my flesh as he moved me up and down faster, creating more friction for his cock, driving himself to the edge and over until he spilled himself up into me.

"You're incredible," he told me.

I smiled down at him. "So are you." Absolutely incredible. And as much mine as the other guys.

"Can you handle one more?" Ramsey asked as Jay helped me off his hips.

"I'd be offended if you didn't," I told him.

Ramsey sat facing me. He grabbed my hands and pulled me forward until my legs were draped over his thighs, his cock positioned outside the entrance to my pussy. Pulling me forward a little more, he slid into me, his piercing massaging me all the way through. His thumb circling my clit, he fucked me, his gaze going from my face to where we were joined and back again.

"I like seeing my dick going into you," he said.

I glanced down to watch. "I like it too." The guys were right, this was exactly what I needed. What work? Right here and now, nothing mattered but me and them. Maybe nothing else had to matter ever again. Could we stay here until the end of time and fuck? That sounded like a good plan to me.

"Come for me," he insisted. "I know you have another one in you."

I wasn't sure if I did, but when he put it that way, I wanted to obey him.

"Yes, sir," I whispered. I started to close my eyes, but he made a sound in the back of his throat.

"Look at me," he insisted. "Look at me and come."

I locked my eyes on his and let another orgasm wrap itself around me and drag me under, into depths I'd never known existed before. I was engulfed and washed away in a world of hot, wet bliss.

He followed a few moments later, thrusting quickly as he lost himself in me. "I fucking love you," he said mid-orgasm. "You're everything and then some."

"I fucking love you too," I said as I started to float back down to earth. "All of you." By now, I was completely boneless and covered in a sheen of sweat. Satisfied as hell.

We flopped forward together, holding each other and trying to catch our breath.

"We need to get you washed up," he whispered finally.

All I could do was murmur my agreement and let them scrape me up off the mattress to take me to the bathroom.

Chapter Two

Chelsea

I STEPPED OUT OF THE SHOWER AND QUICKLY dried myself. I was a little stiff and sore from the thorough fucking, but satisfied as hell. I was very ready for the meal the guys were preparing, and an early night.

Tomorrow, I'd figure out what I was going to do with the rest of my life. Now the world knew what I used to do for a living, no sports team was going to hire me. No general practices either. I could set up my own, but I'd probably struggle to get patients through the door. I'd be lucky if I was allowed to attend my own graduation ceremony.

Maybe it would all blow over; until then, I had no choice but to come up with a plan B. Right now, I couldn't begin to think what that was. I'd have to give myself a few days grace. Or a few weeks maybe. I'd figure things out, I always had before. I needed to get through the next few days first.

I hung the towel up on a hook in the bathroom and stepped into the bedroom to quickly get dressed. I didn't know when, but at some point Frost had clothes in my size delivered to his cottage. Apart from scaring the shit out of me earlier, they were the most thoughtful guys. A girl couldn't ask for better.

Dressed in comfortable track pants, a long sleeved T-shirt and a Smashers hoodie, paired with thick socks that looked like something my brother would have bought for me, I stepped out into the living area.

"So, then he said, I don't care how many laps your coach made you run, he's not here anymore," Frost was saying. "And we said—" He stopped to look over at me and smiled softly. "Hey, we have a guest."

"Yeah, I can see that. Coach Stanley, you're looking well." And very much alive. Curious, considering Dominic King had Storm and Atlas kill the man for him.

"Please, call me Max." He held out his hand.

I shook it and glanced over to Storm and Atlas. "I thought you..."

Storm snorted. "We weren't going to kill the best

head coach we've ever had. We brought him out here so he could hide until we dealt with all the shit back in Dusk Bay."

"Which I'm grateful for," Max said.

"There's another cottage on the property," Frost supplied. "We figured we should invite him over to fill him in on things."

How far away was that cottage? None of us were trying to be quiet while we fucked. If the expression on his face was any indication, he'd heard plenty, but was happy to pretended he hadn't. That suited me. I wasn't ashamed of anything we did, but I didn't necessarily need him overhearing either.

"I'm sorry you got caught up in all of this." I slid into a stool at the kitchen island.

He shrugged. "I'm not going to pretend I'm happy about any of it, but they could have killed me and tossed me into a shallow grave. I count myself lucky my players are loyal. They were just telling me you were fired." He looked regretful.

"I suppose I should be glad I'm not in a shallow grave too," I said on a sigh. "Apparently a public shaming was enough."

"For what it's worth, I don't see how your past job has anything to do with being a team doctor," he said.

"The players all respect you. You're good at what you do. They'll come to realise that."

"I think it's for the best," Frost said. When I looked at him sharply, he continued. "I like it better when you're not in the vicinity of King or Skinner. I'm starting to think we should have stashed you here with Coach weeks ago."

"You think I would have let myself be stashed?" I nodded thanks to Atlas as he placed a bowl of steaming soup in front of me. It smelled delicious, full of potatoes and other vegetables.

"You would have if I said so," Storm said. "I should have. Letting you stay there with the team was a mistake."

"May I remind you, it wasn't your call," Ramsey said. He was in the kitchen cutting open bread rolls with a knife that looked sharper than it needed to be. "That order came from way above both our heads."

"I don't give a shit," Storm told him. "If I wanted Chelsea hidden, she'd be hidden. If they didn't like it, they could fuck all the way off. I don't take orders from them."

"Yes, you do." Ramsey tossed the rolls onto a plate and placed it on the island, within reach. "Whether you like it or not, you do."

"Not when it comes to Chelsea and her safety,"

Storm insisted. "Then I only take orders from myself. I don't care who I have to piss off. She's my priority. Her and the rest of you." His expression softened slightly when he looked at me, then at Frost. The other four were his brothers, he had the softest spot for the two of us.

Frost frowned at Ramsey. "Would you really put her at risk just to follow orders?"

"At risk, no," Ramsey replied. "I did my best to make sure she wasn't. But the bridge you would have burned trying to do your own thing would have burnt you."

"Ramsey is right," I said quickly when Storm and Frost opened their mouths to argue with him. "I was safe and it's not worth making enemies of the Brantley family. I might have avoided ending up in my brother's workroom, hanging from chains, but I can't guarantee the same for any of you." He wouldn't have liked it, but if he had no choice, that's what Ice would have done.

"Is it weird I'm a little turned on by that?" Frost asked.

"Not even a little bit," I told him. "When we get home, I can chain you up in our basement if you like."

"I'd like that," he said with barely contained glee,

that he dialled back when he remembered Max was in the room. He looked over to him, an awkward smile on his face.

Max responded with a chuckle and indulgent shake of his head, his dark hair flopping onto his forehead. "If you think you can say anything that would surprise me, think again. I've been around rugby players all my life. There's not much I haven't heard or seen. Or done. I won't lie, the whole mafia thing was something I didn't anticipate, but I should have. I was aware Dusk Bay had a dark side. Darker than other cities. I was naïve, and thought they wouldn't infiltrate the team. Of course they would. They did the same with the Demons, why not us?"

I leaned over to quickly pat his arm. "Don't feel too bad about it. They were a lot more subtle with the Smashers than they were with the Demons. I'm not even sure the owner is aware."

Ramsey cleared his throat.

I sighed. "That answers that then. Is their last name Brantley? Or Bell? Maybe Lasalle or DiMarco?"

"Mack D'Antonio," Ramsey said. "He's a close friend of Reuben Brantley. If anyone could consider themselves close to him. When it comes to the team, he keeps a low profile. Officially, he's a businessman and the team is just another asset. It's likely he doesn't care too much what happens to the team, or at the stadium."

"He knows who King and Skinner are though, right?" Frost asked.

"He'd be aware, yes," Ramsey agreed. "That backs up my thought that Reuben wants them to make a move. He's letting them get comfortable before he destroys them."

"Or he doesn't care either." Storm scowled.

"That's possible," Ramsey conceded. "At least, about the team. He's not going to let them get a firm foothold in Dusk Bay."

Max raised his hand. "Can I ask a question? What can I do? I don't want to let these people destroy our team."

"You wait," Ramsey said. "While they think you're dead, you're safe. When this is over, the team will need its head coach back."

"I hope you have some logical explanation for my disappearance," Max said. "And subsequent return from the dead."

"It was a miracle," Frost said, holding out his hands in front of him, fingers splayed.

"It's a good question," Storm said. "What are we going to tell people?"

"Max had a bout with a 'serious illness,'" Ramsey said. "He had a miraculous recovery."

"How are we going to explain the body in the burnt out car?" Storm insisted. "He was already dead," he said before anyone could ask.

"Mistaken identity," Ramsey said easily. "He stole Max's car and got into an accident. Any other questions, we'll figure out later."

"You boys went to a lot of trouble to keep from killing me," Max said gratefully. "I appreciate that."

"Nothing you wouldn't have done for us," Storm said gruffly. "Besides, Atlas might have been able to kill you, but I couldn't. I don't want to go around killing people if I can help it."

"Lucky they didn't send Frost," Jay said. "He might have done it." He sat quietly until now, eating his soup and roll, and listening to the rest of us talk.

"Not to Coach," Frost protested. "I offered up my cottage, remember?"

"I might have remembered if I knew about this before half an hour ago," Jay said. He turned to me and added, "They left me and Dallas out of it." His tone was tight, like he'd been quietly seething, gathering his thoughts, and now he was ready to let them out.

"You were grieving," Atlas said. "If you knew

what we did, you wouldn't have been so convincing." He cocked his head at Jay, brow creased as though somehow surprised by his boyfriend's response.

"Maybe I would have." Jay squinted at Atlas. "Did it cross your mind to let me make that call? Or did you want to keep it a secret?" His dark eyes were laced with hurt and anger. He was as blindsided as I was.

Should I be angry too? Possibly, but I wasn't. I was happy to see Max and more than a little relieved Storm and Atlas hadn't killed him. They'd taken a huge risk though. Failing to follow an order like that could have gotten them killed. Keeping it from the rest of us wouldn't have been easy.

For his part, Dallas didn't look even slightly bothered. Yes, they lied, but with good reason. That was the past, he'd already moved on from it. Knowing him, he was probably thinking about fucking me, not worrying about what the other guys had or hadn't done.

"Babe, I didn't want to lie to you." Atlas draped an arm over Jay's shoulders. "The fewer people who knew, the better. What if they suspected and asked you outright? Would you have been able to look them in the eyes and lie to them?" He silently pleaded with Jay to understand and forgive him.

Fuck knew we already had enough conflict between us, without this damaging what they had.

"We'll never know." Jay stepped away from him. "You didn't give me the chance. I thought you trusted me." He crossed his arms and firmed his jaw. Classic defensive posture, wanting physical and emotional distance between him and Atlas.

My heart hurt to see it. Was there anything I could say or do to help him understand? Honestly, I wasn't sure he'd be receptive to words from anyone right now. He needed to take a few moments and calm down. Then he might be ready to think rationally and listen. At least, I hoped he would.

Frost reached out a hand to Jay, but he jerked away from him too, leaving the other player to drop his arm and step back a little, giving him some space.

"Jay, I do trust you. Of course I do," Atlas started. "Not about that, it's—"

The lights flickered a couple of times before they went out, plunging us into darkness.

Chapter Three

Ramsey

I IMMEDIATELY FROZE. EVERY SENSE WAS ON high alert. The only sound inside the cottage was the guys around me, and Chelsea, breathing, somebody swearing softly and the ticking of a clock.

"Stay still," I whispered. "Nobody move yet. Not until I tell you to."

I wasn't sure if they'd do what I said, especially Storm and Atlas, both who prided themselves on their alpha masculinity. Storm in particular, liked being in control of all of us.

If this was something more than a harmless power outage, then it was me who needed to be in charge. This sort of situation was my territory. More so than theirs. They were catching on quickly, but they didn't have the experience I did.

Okay, maybe there was some ego involved too. I wanted to keep Chelsea safe. Especially after we scared the shit out of her by kidnapping her unexpectedly. It seemed like a good idea at the time, but maybe we should have thought it through a bit more.

That couldn't be helped now.

"What do we do?" Frost whispered back.

"Stay put," I said. "Stay quiet."

Storm grumbled something under his breath, but didn't argue. Yet.

Silently, I stepped away from the kitchen island and moved to the front of the house. The curtains were closed, but a small gap allowed me to peer out.

The night was pitch dark, broken only by a distant light from the cottage Max Stanley was hiding out in.

Fuck.

Not a power outage then.

The clouds shifted overhead, letting the moon illuminate part of the forest a hundred or so metres from the house. And a couple of figures moving through the darkness.

Double fuck.

I turned back and bumped into someone. Barely managed to keep from making a noise of surprise.

"It's me," Frost whispered. So much for staying

put. "I stashed a few weapons in the spare room, in case we needed them."

"We need them," I said. I put a hand on his bicep and let him guide me to the spare room and the cupboard set into the wall.

"Is this where you tell me I can't use my phone to show you?" he asked.

"No phones," I agreed. I peeled back enough curtain to let in the moonlight. It slanted across a box of guns and knives.

A few weapons? It looked like he was preparing for the Apocalypse.

"Nice work." I picked the box up, grunting under the weight, and carried it to the kitchen. Placing it down on the wooden kitchen table, I started to hand out weapons, checking each to make sure they were loaded.

"I've never used one," Max said as I handed him a handgun.

"If anyone points a gun at you, point that end at them and pull the trigger," I instructed. "Make sure you don't shoot one of us." That was as much advice as we had time for right now. If we got through this, I'd happily give him more.

"Do you know who it is?" Chelsea asked softly. She took a gun without flinching, even though I knew she didn't want to use one. She was the strong-est, most beautiful woman I ever met. Much stronger than she gave herself credit for.

I wished I could have kept her from this, but I couldn't. There was an inevitability about it that was out of my control. Not just because the Brantley family wanted her back into the fold, but because she belonged to this life more than she was prepared to admit. She wasn't going to go and hide in a cupboard and let us deal with whoever was coming. She'd stand back to back with the rest of us until the end.

"No, but I have a few guesses," I said. "Everyone get down and start heading for the back door." I didn't want to get pinned down in here if we could help it.

The moonlight was fainter in here, but I made out Frost, crouched beside me. "I don't suppose you have a secret tunnel anywhere in this place?"

"Not that I know of," he said. "I'll be sure to have one added after this."

I nodded. That sucked, but it was what it was. The mansion had one. More than one. We could have escaped through one of them and been gone before anyone noticed.

Here, we'd have to be careful.

Keeping to the back of the pack, I followed the others to the back door.

"Are we making a run for it?" Storm whispered, loud enough to make me wince.

"If it's safe." I worked my way around them to crouch beside him. "Open the door as quietly as you can."

He grunted, but did what I told him to, working the lock open with a soft click. He placed his hand on the handle and turned it slowly, easing the door open inward.

"There's someone out there," he said, more softly this time.

"Yeah," I agreed. Several someones. They had us surrounded. "Stay here. When they move away, run. Head for the forest and lose yourself in the trees."

"What are you gonna do?" Atlas asked.

I didn't answer. I rose to my feet and walked back to the front of the house, making no attempt to quiet my footsteps. I took out my phone and turned on the light before I unlocked the front door and pulled it open.

My gun down low, I moved the phone around, as if trying to figure out the source of the power outage. I kept the device in front of me, so the light would mask my identity, for now.

A male voice shouted and a couple of them converged on my position.

"What is this?" I demanded. Now was not the time to show fear. I was an innocent man who rented out this lovely, peaceful cottage for a couple of nights.

Okay, chances were, they weren't going to buy that. A guy could try.

"Ferris Ramsey, who are you trying to bullshit?"

I turned the light and shone it right into Carlos Jones' eyes.

"Fuck." He put a hand up in front of his face. "You got a death wish?"

Slowly, and with no apology, I lowered the device. "Not tonight. Since when does the head of the Crimson Vipers come out to a place like this?" Especially in person.

"Since you have something I want," he said evenly.

"I'm flattered, but not interested," I said dryly. We both knew he wasn't talking about me, but I needed to keep him distracted so the others could sneak away. I'd keep him here for as long as possible. Even if he killed me for it. For a long time, I knew I might die to keep Chelsea safe. And the others. It was what I signed up for and what I'd take if that's how this went down. In the scheme of things, I was no one important. Just another lackey. Jones would kill me without a second thought or hint of regret.

He snorted. "You're not my type. If you were, I'd just insist. You do work for me, after all. Right?"

"Of course I do," I said. "If I have something you want, why not just ask?" We both knew it wasn't that simple. Even if I was loyal to him, I wasn't giving up my woman, not without a fight. I'd die first, but I preferred he be the one to do the dying.

"I was asking myself the same question," he said easily. "I said to myself, Carlos, why are you going to all this effort? Why not just take what you want, like you always do? And you know what the answer was?"

"What was it?" I asked. I might as well humour him if it kept him busy for a while longer. The distraction wouldn't last for long, I knew that. He was too smart to fall for it.

"The answer was, I don't believe you're working for me." His tone turned more dangerous. "I believe your loyalty is where it's always been: the Brantley family."

"The same place your loyalty is, right?" I asked. Two could play that game.

He barked a laugh. "My loyalty is with me. The

Brantley family were useful, but I'm not really sure they are any more. I think it's time they were replaced."

"By you?" I asked, although I already knew the answer.

"Of course by me. Now is the time to have the right allegiance." He laced his fingers in front of himself. "You can pledge your loyalty to me and keep on living, or you can die alongside the rest of the Brantleys." He might have been asking if I preferred vanilla ice cream to chocolate. For the record, I don't. Chocolate is by far the superior flavour. Although, it paled in comparison to the taste of Chelsea's pussy.

"I have no desire to die for them," I said. I didn't want to work for him either, but I'd play along for now. "You still haven't told me what it is you want." As much fun as this stupid game was, I was becoming bored with it. I preferred the direct approach. Jones, unfortunately, always seemed to prefer the dramatic one. As if sneaking up in the dark of night added an exotic flair to the evening's event. If you've asked me, he was playing a stupid game and deserved a stupid prize for it. Top of my list was a bullet in his brain.

"Let me tell you a story." He tapped the tips of his fingers against his thigh. "I used to frequent a little club in the city called Flirts. Have you heard of it?"

My blood iced over. "I have."

"Then you know they have the most beautiful women in the country working there. Dancing and fucking. There was one in particular. A brunette with legs for days and a pierced clit. She danced like a cat, so lithe and flexible. Her ass was so tight I could bite into it like a peach." He raised his hand to his mouth, miming doing just that. He seemed amused, knowing he was getting to me bit by bit. I tried to keep my annoyance off my face, but apparently failed. And he was enjoying every moment of it.

He went on. "Her breasts were the kind a man dreams about fucking. Right before coming on her face." He grabbed his groin and grinned.

"I don't pay to fuck women, but I might have made an exception for her. But then she left the club. Such a terrible shame." He clicked his tongue. "I've waited long enough to have her. I won't wait any more. She belongs to me and I've come to claim her."

I wanted to shoot him in the middle of his face for having seen Chelsea naked, dancing on that stage. Even if he hadn't touched her, his eyes had feasted on her body. Her ass, her breasts, her nipples.

All of them belonged to me and her other boyfriends. Not to a snake like this. I kept the gun down, trying to look as nonthreatening as possible. Had I given the others enough time to get clear yet? I wasn't sure. Another couple of minutes might be just enough. I may never see Chelsea again, but I'd do whatever I could to make sure she was safe.

I shrugged one shoulder. "I'm sorry, but that sounds like several of the women from Flirts. Divina only hires the best. You might have to be more specific." I sent a silent apology to Chelsea. None of the other girls came close to holding a candle to her. She was in a league of her own. Honestly, it wasn't that surprising she caught his eye. Wherever she went, people stared at her, lusted after her.

Jones took a few steps closer. He started to look irritated. He knew that I knew exactly who he was referring to and he was done playing with me. Like a cat with a mouse, he was ready to bite me in two and discard my remains.

"She used to dance under the name of Sparkle. You know her as Doctor Chelsea Miller. I know she's here with you. Hand her over to me and you might get to live."

Chapter Four

Chelsea

"You know that asshat?" Storm growled softly.

"I remember him from Flirts," I whispered. "He used to stand at the back of the crowds and watch."

"That was all he did?" Atlas asked.

We all knew why he was asking that. If it was anything more, chances were he was about to shoot off Carlos' cock.

"That was all," I agreed. "We should get out of here."

I hated leaving Ramsey here to face these people alone. As far as I could tell, most of them moved around the front when he appeared.

I wasn't naïve enough to think all of them had.

"Let's go," Storm looked back towards Ramsey

with the same expression of regret. Gun in one hand, he gestured for us to move ahead of him.

"Keep your eyes peeled for bad guys," Atlas said.

Any belief that we were working with them would be out the window the moment Ramsey refused to hand me over to Carlos Jones. We'd immediately become the enemy. They wouldn't hesitate to kill us, even me.

"How do we know if they're a bad guy?" Max asked tentatively.

"Because they aim at us," Atlas told him. "Don't hesitate. They won't."

"Shit," Max said under his breath. He held his gun in both hands, aimed toward the ground. Just like they did in action movies when they had no real idea how to hold one.

I would have told him to raise it, but a nervous person with a gun at the same level as my face was a bad idea. Better he keep it down low for now.

We headed into the deepest shadows and trotted towards the trees, moving as silently as we could. Gravel and sticks scrunched under our shoes, making me wince and hope like hell they didn't sound as loud as I was perceiving. To me, they sounded like landmines exploding with every step. Noise so loud it would be heard in Dusk Bay.

I held my breath until wide trunks and the heavy canopy created a deeper darkness around us. Enveloping us and helping us to disappear.

"No one seems to be coming for us," Frost said, sounding unconvinced.

"No, they don't." I frowned. Either they hadn't seen us, or Jones was so confident the guys would give me to him, that he hadn't bothered to ensure we were fully surrounded.

Something about this was off. There was no way in hell it was this easy.

"I'm going to circle back around the front," Atlas said. "If they try anything with Ramsey..."

"I'm coming with you," I said. The hair on the back of my neck started to stand up. Fear was slowly getting the better of me. I wanted to be anywhere but here.

Not to mention I wouldn't be able to live with myself if anything happened to Ramsey because of me.

"Me too," Frost said.

"And me," Jay whispered. He seemed to have calmed down now.

I guessed in the face of things, his anger at Atlas had lessened. That whole conversation seemed like nothing important now. Barely a blip on the radar.

"We're all going." Storm slipped ahead through the trees, leaving the rest of us to catch up.

Not an easy task, given it was pitch black, and fallen trunks and twigs made trip hazards here and there. The only saving grace was that the leaves were wet underfoot, squelching softly rather than crunching and snapping.

A hand slipped into mine, and I was pulled close to Dallas' side.

"I won't let anything happen to you," he said near my ear. His words were confident, but he sounded as anxious as I felt.

"I won't let anything happen to you either," I whispered back. Not if I could help it.

Could I help it? That was the question. Would it be easier to give myself to Jones than risk all of these guys? What could he do to me that I hadn't already done? If he wanted me to dance for him, then for him to fuck me, hadn't I done that for years?

It was always my choice before, but it was also my choice to make sure these incredible men got out of here alive.

Before I could act on that, the air was split with Jones' growl of irritation.

"You'd die for a piece of pussy?" he demanded.

Ramsey's voice was louder now, continuing to

distract the cartel leader as best as he could. "If you thought Chelsea Miller was just a piece of pussy, you wouldn't be here."

Doctor, I mentally corrected him. Although, I supposed that side of me didn't much matter anymore. Not if I could never practice medicine again. Still, I earned that title and I'd continue to own it.

"You're right," Jones said smoothly. "She's more than a piece of pussy. She's *my* piece of pussy. That much should be clear by now."

"How would it be clear?" Ramsey asked. "Have your people been the ones taking pot shots at her?"

"Not at her," Jones growled. "The first time, the gunshot was meant to be a distraction. She was supposed to be grabbed and brought to me."

I swallowed hard. Ramsey guessed at the possibility, but not who was ultimately behind it.

"And the second time?" Ramsey asked. "Was Milly supposed to kill Sierra as a distraction as well?"

Carlos actually growled in response. "That had nothing to do with me. If I find out who hired that little bitch, I'm going to have them sold to some particularly vicious people I know. It was probably one of the Brantley assholes. Look for a pair of twins, they're usually involved in shit like that. I should have them sold too."

I smirked to myself. It was unlikely he or any of his people would get close enough to Hunter and Parker Brantley to traffic them anywhere. I also didn't buy that they had anything to do with Milly killing Sierra. It was the kind of thing they did, yes, but my gut feeling told me it wasn't them. Who was it? I wasn't sure.

Honestly, I could guess all day and not pin down exactly who it was and why.

"We can agree on that then," Ramsey said. "We didn't appreciate anyone waving a gun around Chelsea either." His tone got darker, clearly referencing the fact that Jones had a bunch of armed men here outside the cottage. He sounded ready to shoot them all himself.

"I don't give a fuck what you didn't appreciate," Jones snapped. "You have thirty seconds to give her to me or I'll put a bullet in your brain."

My grip on my gun tightened. If I was to surrender myself to him, would he let Ramsey live? Men like him often gave no fucks about keeping their word. You know what they say, there's no honour amongst thieves. Especially a lowlife like Carlos Jones. I'd sooner dance naked in the middle of

Smashers Stadium than trust a thing he said. He could bundle me into the back of a car and kill all of them anyway.

"No," Dallas whispered. "I know what you're thinking and I'm not letting you do it."

"We can't let him kill Ramsey," I insisted.

"You're not going with that asshole." He was just as insistent.

"I'm not sure there's any other way." I shook my head. "All of you need to get out of here alive. The team needs you."

"Fuck the team," he grunted. "I need you. I don't want to fucking live without you. If they take you, I better be dead first."

"Dallas..." What could I say to that? "I love you. You would be okay without me. I promise." It would hurt a little at first, but he'd move on eventually. He had a lot of love to give. He'd find someone else to give it to. I hated the idea, but it was better than thinking of him dead or lonely.

"I'd die either way," he said. "I'd shrivel up and die like a fish out of the ocean. I'd probably smell like one too."

I doubted that, but I understood where he was coming from. I'd probably want to shrivel up too if anything happened to these guys.

"Twenty seconds," Jones called out. He turned around slowly, as if he knew we were there, but not exactly where.

"I have to," I said. I had no choice. I wasn't going to let anyone sacrifice themselves for me. I wouldn't.

I tried to pull away from Dallas, but he grabbed my wrist and held on hard.

His grip would leave bruises, but I couldn't bring myself to try to push him off. If I did, he might lose his shit. I felt desperation and fear coming off him in waves. He was absolutely certain he couldn't exist without me in his life, beside him as much as possible. Fucking me every chance he had. Lying in bed at night, his cock deep inside me as we slept.

"Chelsea." He sounded devastated I'd even consider walking away from him.

"Ten seconds." Jones stopped to face Ramsey again.

My heart raced. This was what I feared when I was lying in the back of the car as the guys drove me here. That someone like him had taken me and I'd never see them again.

This way, I got to decide for myself. I'd make the sacrifice if I had to.

"I don't know where she is." Ramsey raised and

lowered his spare hand, letting it slap against his jeans clad thigh.

"That's unfortunate for you," Carlos said. "I'm at the end of my patience."

"I'm not having the time of my life either," Ramsey said. "Fortunately, we were able to keep you talking long enough to have everyone in place. You and all the lackeys you brought with you are surrounded. I'll give you one chance to get the hell out of here, or you'll be the one with a bullet in your brain."

"He means us," Frost whispered excitedly.

"Yeah, he does." Storm sounded less excited. "I guess we better not let him down."

Still holding my wrist tightly, Dallas drew me along with him, following the others as we stepped out of the trees.

Chapter Five

Chelsea

"It appears to me you lied," Jones said, dark eyes on me as I appeared in the light from his vehicle. "Miss Miller seems to be very much right here."

"Doctor Miller," I corrected.

"So she does," Ramsey agreed.

"You can't have her," Storm growled. "You might as well get back in your car and fuck off right now."

Jones clicked his tongue. "Storm Keller. Is that any way to talk to the new owner of the Dusk Bay Smashers?"

Storm did a double take. "Bullshit. You don't own the team. Even if you did, you're not taking my woman."

"Our woman," Atlas said.

"Argue another time," Jay told them.

"You don't own the Smashers," Ramsey said.

Without taking his eyes off me, Jones smiled. "Not yet, but soon. I look forward to replacing all of you."

Frost snorted derisively. "Good luck with that. First of all, we don't believe you're getting your hands on the team. Secondly, the team is winning with us. Unless you want to lose."

"You're not the only, or even the best, players in the country," Jones sneered. "If you behave, I might let you stay. I can give... Doctor Miller her job back."

"Why would you do that?" I asked. Clearly he wanted something in return. I suspected the price would be too high for me to pay. My soul, perhaps? My body, definitely.

"Why would I not want the best working for me?" he asked.

"You just said you want to trade us out," Frost said.

Jones' gaze slid to him. "Who said anything about trading you? I said I wanted to replace you."

"I think he means he plans to kill us," Storm said. He sounded unimpressed.

"You know, I think you're right," Frost said. "I find

that even more objectionable. Also unlikely. I don't know if you know anything about football, but usually if one team has more guys on the field than the other, they tend to win. It's called a numbers advantage. Have you heard of it?"

Jones glared at him, his eyes narrowed.

I thought back to the last time I saw him in Flirts, watching me disappear into a room with Storm and Dallas. He gave me the creeps then. That hadn't changed one bit.

What would I have done if he approached me back then? I would have had Divina's support to tell him no, but would he have come after me like this if I had?

Back then, I wasn't surrounded by six muscular rugby players. I would have been a much easier target. Why hadn't he made his move then? I supposed because people would have noticed me not turning up to work. Now, they wouldn't give a shit. I had no work to turn up to.

"I'm sure you're also well aware that a professional team, even with a numbers advantage, would destroy an amateur one," Jones said. "Do any of you even know how to use a gun?"

"I do," I said. "Give me one good reason why I shouldn't shoot you right now."

"Because you want to return to the Smashers," he said. "I'm your only chance of doing that. Once the sale is finalised, I'll tell the press the report they published was all a pack of lies. They got you mixed up with someone else. You can get on with your life, treating the players. I'll even make sure you replace Doctor Stuart when he retires."

"You're not thinking about doing that, are you?" Dallas asked frantically.

"Of course she's not," Storm snapped. "Get a grip."

"What would you want in return?" I called out.

"You," he said. "That's all. You can get on with your life, more or less. The one thing that would change is you'd be mine. I'm a reasonable man. Also a very rich one. I can give you everything you want and need."

"As long as I'm your fuck toy," I stated.

He responded with a brief laugh at the back of his throat. "If you want to put it like that, yes. Surely that would be better than being a fuck toy for six meat heads?" He gestured around to the guys.

"Rude," Frost remarked. "Anyway, Chelsea is not a toy. She loves us and we love her, right, Chels?"

I thought back to when Storm and I met. He told

me then that I was his fuck toy. That I belonged to him and would do what he told me to do.

At the time, I hadn't minded, Now, the memory, and hearing it from Jones, hit hard.

For so long, that was all I was. All I saw myself as. Just a body for men to stare at and fuck. I'd loved every minute of it, but right now I felt pared down to nothing but an object.

Dallas pulled me closer, trembling hand still gripping my wrist. "Chels? You're not a fuck toy. You're a fucking goddess. We all worship you, body, heart and mind. I won't let anyone treat you differently." He was almost begging now. Pleading for me to stay with him.

"Me either," Jay said. "Can I kill this prick now?" He waved his gun in the general direction of Jones.

"Same question," Frost said. "I know you love working for the team, but you're not going to let yourself be used by him, right?"

"Of course she's not," Storm snapped. "What sort of dumbass question is that?"

"Judging by the look on her face, a reasonable one," Jones said. "She can come with me willingly, or over all of your dead bodies." He nodded and his minions stepped in closer, guns pointed at us.

"You're still out—" Frost stopped mid-sentence as

several other minions stepped out of the cars behind Jones'. "Fuck."

Jones chuckled. "You were saying? It seems to me that I have the numbers advantage. Assuming you can count past six."

"This guy is starting to piss me off," Storm growled. "For one thing, there's eight of us, dickhead. In case *you* can't count that high."

"That doesn't change the fact there are now a twelve well-trained guns aimed at you," Jones said without flinching. "You might take out one or two, but none of you will walk away. Not unless Chelsea comes with me right now. If she does, I'll let all of you go. I'm sure it won't take you long to find another pussy to fuck. I'm surprised you shared at all, much less for this long. I won't be sharing her with anyone."

"Chelsea," Dallas pleaded again. "Please don't."

"What choice do I have?" I whispered. "If I don't go with him, all of you will be dead. He'll take me anyway."

"I'd rather be dead," he whispered.

"He's right," I said. "You'll find someone else. Forget all about me and get on with your lives."

"With you working for the team?" Frost asked, looking confused.

"I won't go back there," I said.

I knew how this would really go down. None of them would ever see me again. Not at the stadium, not at a game, nowhere. I'd never see any of their faces again, for as long as I lived. These were our last moments together.

They had to be. I couldn't let them be killed for me. Not when they had lives to live.

"You can't be serious?" Storm snarled. "There's no fucking way you're going with him. Let him kill us, if he can. I'm not letting this happen."

"It doesn't seem to me like you have a choice," Jones said easily. "She's made hers. Be a good boy and respect it."

Storm let out a bark-laugh so loud, I flinched. "I haven't been a good boy yet and I don't intend to start trying. Eat shit, asshole." He raised his gun and aimed it at Jones.

"Wait." Ramsey trotted down the front steps of the cottage to stand approximately between us and Jones. "I'm sure we can end this without bloodshed."

"I prefer bloodshed," Storm said. His hand was unwavering, still aiming carefully.

"Ramsey is right," I said. "No one needs to die here today."

"I'm okay with this asshole leaving right now," Storm said.

"Me too." Atlas raised his own gun and aimed it at the cartel leader.

Jones rolled his eyes and shook his head. "Atlas Underwood. I have to admit, you did a good job of pretending to be on their side. Even I was convinced for a while there." He started to clap slowly. "This is going to be quite the blow to the Brantley family. You would have been a valuable asset for them. What a shame you're loyal to me instead."

I stared at Atlas at the same time Storm said, "What the fuck?"

Jones continued. "You can stop pretending now. You and Jayden Lang there. You've done a commendable job infiltrating these... people. I need you back with me now."

"First our intelligence, now our humanity," Frost grumbled. "This asshole really knows how to insult people." He held his own gun loosely in his hand. Ready, but not entirely certain which direction to aim it. He clearly didn't want to accept that Atlas was working for Jones, any more than I did. It made no sense, but at the same time it made too much sense.

My heart was cracking right down the middle. Atlas and Jay used all of us. Right from the start, everything they said was a lie. To think I trusted them, gave myself to them. Right now, I wanted to throw up on their shoes. Or shoot them both in the head.

"Not insulting, just stating facts," Jones said, seemingly oblivious to the turmoil in my mind.

"Thanks, boss." Atlas lowered the gun.

Jay looked over at him sharply, but didn't protest.

"I might even reconsider sharing Chelsea," Jones said smoothly. "She seems to like both of you."

My stomach turned harder.

Frost looked white as a sheet. He stared at Jay and Atlas like he'd never seen either of them before. He didn't even try to hide his hurt. They might as well rip his heart out and stomp all over it.

If that was a lie, what else was? I was starting to question everything I thought I knew.

Atlas glanced over at Jay and nodded. "It's about time. I'm sick of pretending to like these dickheads." He stepped away from us and turned to aim his gun at Storm's face.

After a moment, Jay followed him.

"What the fuck?" Frost gaped at them. "You can't be fucking serious?"

Jay looked pained, but Atlas turned his gaze to me and jerked his head towards Jones' car. "Let's go."

"No," Dallas groaned. "Please."

"He could be useful, boss," Atlas said over his shoulder. "He was the one who killed India."

"Bring him then," Jones said after a few moments of contemplation.

Dallas looked from me to Storm, to Atlas and back to me. "Wherever she goes, I go."

"You fucking suck," Frost told him. He was starting to look defeated. His shoulders slumped, gun still hanging from his fingers.

Storm shook his head. "This isn't happening."

"It's happening," Atlas told him. "Chelsea." His face was a mask, cold and expressionless. He barely looked like the man I knew. Thought I knew. This man was a complete stranger. Worse than a stranger. He was the enemy. He had been all along. What else had he done to us? What had Jay done to us?

I didn't want to look at either of them. All this time, they'd been working for the other side, pretending to be with us? Pretending to care about me? Had I really been that stupid? Yes, apparently I had. Stupid, blind and in love with someone who didn't give a shit about me.

My heart ached like hell. I clung on to Dallas while I stepped over to the car and slipped into the back seat.

Dallas crowded in beside me, sitting as close as

he could. Jay sat on the other side, keeping a safer distance.

I glanced out the window at Frost's devastated face, as he stood between Ramsey and Storm, Max Stanley behind them, watching us drive away.

Chapter Six

Ramsey

"That was bullshit." Storm lowered his gun, but looked like he was ready to shoot the next person or thing that pissed him off.

Frost shook his head. He looked completely bewildered. "What the hell happened? Why would they do that us?"

"Because they're fucking pricks," Storm snarled. "I told you Atlas was an asshole. Right from the very fucking beginning, I told all of you. And you—" He pointed the gun at me.

"You wanted us to get along with each other. You too." He swivelled his upper body to aim the gun at Max. "Get along," he sneered. "Be a team. Look where that fucking got us."

Frost grabbed his wrist and pushed the gun down. "You're not going to shoot Coach or Ramsey."

"Give me one good reason why not." Storm jerked his arm away. "They let this happen. Ramsey let this fucking happen."

I gazed back at him evenly. Frost was right, he wasn't going to shoot me. If he tried, I was ready. Faster and more accurate than him. I didn't want to kill him, but I wasn't going to let him kill me because he let his anger get the better of him.

"I didn't let this happen," I said.

I was cool and calm on the outside, but on the inside I was as furious as Storm. I should have stopped this from happening. I should have known Jones would find us here. He would have been having at least one of us followed, waiting for an opportunity like this. We never should have brought Chelsea here, it made her vulnerable. All of us got caught up making her feel better and now we were paying the price for that. She was paying the price.

"I'm not going to stand by while it does," I added. "We need to get out of here and regroup. We need backup. Then we can go after her."

Mentally, I added, 'and Dallas.' I wasn't sure what game Atlas and Jay were playing, but Dallas couldn't look past his obsession with Chelsea. This wasn't about loyalty to Jones over us. This was about his feelings for her and his inability to comprehend being away from her.

To be honest, I could relate completely. I didn't want to be away from her either, but I had to be the one to take control now. To get us out of here and come up with a solid plan.

"Ice is going to be murderous," Frost said with barely contained glee.

It didn't take a genius to know he was picturing Jones in chains in Ice's workroom. Maybe in ours. Either scenario involved blood and pain. And the potential for war between the Crimson Vipers and the Brantley family.

Right now, I couldn't worry about that. My focus was on Chelsea and getting her back before Jones lay a hand on her. If he did, I'd cut it off for him.

"I'm fucking murderous," Storm muttered. "I'm going to start with Atlas fucking Underwood and go from there."

"I can't believe he was working with them all along." Frost tapped his gun against his thigh.

"I should have seen it," I said. "Jones didn't seem surprised to see Max alive and well."

Storm swore, the implication sinking in. "Atlas must have told him what we did."

"Asshole," Frost spat. "If I had a time machine, I'd go back and shoot him in the nuts."

"What now?" Max asked. He looked nervous, standing there in the moonlight beside the cottage with us.

I'd seen him proud, frustrated and angry, but never scared. The things he saw tonight, weren't things he would have seen before. Unless he was also faking. I didn't think he was, though, to be honest. His fear looked genuine.

"First we take you somewhere else," I said. I squinted at my gun before carefully putting on the safety. "Now they know you're alive, they might decide to change that. Then the rest of us are going after our woman."

"Dibs on killing Jay," Frost said softly. "I thought he cared about me. He was just bullshitting, along with Atlas."

"Dibs on Atlas," Storm said darkly. "I want to look him right in the eye and kill his ass."

I was tempted to remind them to wait and see how things played out, because someone else might get to them first. Instead, I pursed my lips and let them have their moment. They had anger they needed to burn off, so let them burn it. They'd be more focused later.

I hoped.

Frost stared at Storm, then swore again. "That's how he found us here, wasn't it? Atlas told him where to look."

"Motherfucker." Storm glared in the direction of the driveway leading out of the property, as though he might shoot lasers far enough to incinerate the inside centre. "I'm going to kill him very, very slowly. I'm going to tie his arms to one car and his legs to the other and we'll drive in opposite directions."

"Three cars," Frost said. "The other one tied to his nuts."

While they burnt off steam discussing the ways they were going to torture and kill Atlas, I surveyed the area. The other two cars had left, taking all of the minions with them. As far as I could tell, there wasn't anyone waiting to jump out at us. If there was, we'd deal with them.

For now though, Jones thought he won. He thought he had his trophy and returned a couple of minions to the fold along the way. Let him enjoy the moment. I was about to rain hell down on his head.

Frost was right, Chelsea's brother would be furious when he found out what happened to her. Jones knew enough about her to know who she was related to. He must have known he was playing with fire, but he struck the match anyway.

Let the others fight over who was going to kill Atlas and Jay. I made myself a promise that I was going to personally take care of Carlos Jones.

"Let's get our stuff." Without waiting to see if they heard, I headed back into the cottage.

The moment I stepped foot back inside, the lights came back on, making me blink against the sudden glare.

Bowls of half-eaten soup and plates of barely touched bread rolls sat where they'd been abandoned.

Chelsea ate most of hers. Good girl. She was going to need her strength to get through the next few hours.

That was as long as her ordeal would last. No longer. By the time the sun set again, she'd be back with me. There were no two ways about that. What would happen if I couldn't pull that off? I didn't want to contemplate it.

Chances were, Jones would try to whisk her off to the other side of the planet. To a place we couldn't find her. Somewhere he could do whatever he wanted to her.

That was absolutely out of the question. She was

far enough from me already. Out of my sight was too far.

I snatched up my bag and hers, pulled the zippers shut before swinging them both over one shoulder. I was halfway back to the car before I realised the others were right behind me.

"I'm going to have bad memories of this cottage now," Frost said. "This was always a nice place to come and hide out from the world. Now, I feel like the world has violated it." He let out a heavy, frustrated sigh.

"Don't use that word," Storm growled. He grabbed the bags one by one and threw them into the back of the SUV, right where Chelsea lay as we drove her here.

If I had a clue what was going to happen, I would have insisted not to doing that to her. I wouldn't have brought her here in the first place. I don't know where I would have taken her, but it wouldn't be here. Frost was right, this place had bad memories now. If I never stepped foot back in the place, that would be all right with me.

"Sorry," Frost said, dropping his face, so his chin almost touched his chest. "Yeah, wrong word. They better not..."

"Yeah, they better not," Storm agreed. "If they

touch a hair on her head, or any part of her..." He shook his head and stomped over to the driver's seat, keys jangling in his hand.

"Wait a minute," I said.

I pulled out my phone, turned on the light and crouched down on the ground beside the vehicle. I turned the light towards the underside of the SUV, moved it slowly across the length of the car from front to back. Satisfied it was safe, I stood back up.

"Did you really just check for explosives?" Max asked, eyes wide. "I feel like I'm living in an action movie."

"That explains the popcorn craving," Frost said. Apparently his sense of humour was intact. Or rather, that was his way of coping with what was going on. I got that. Sometimes dark humour was the only thing that got people through the day or night. I, for one, wouldn't tell him to stop.

I turned off the light and reached for the handle to open the front passenger door. "It pays to be careful. We don't know what they were up to when we were in the trees. The vehicle was out of our sight." If it was me, I would have left a bomb. The fact they hadn't was an oversight on their part. One I was happy to take full advantage of.

"That's kinda badass," Frost said appreciatively. "Are you sure you're not bi?"

I patted him on the shoulder before I slipped into the vehicle. "Sorry, mate, but no. But if I was, I'd be into you."

"Hell yeah you would." He climbed in behind me. "I'm smokin' hot."

"Close the door," Storm snapped. "We've fucked around here for long enough."

Frost said something under his breath, but closed the door harder than was necessary.

"Don't break the—" Storm turned around to growl something at him when the cottage exploded with a loud bang and a burst of flames.

Chapter Seven

Chelsea

We sat in silence as the car headed away from the cottage.

My mind was in turmoil. Disbelief. The only thing keeping me sane right now was Dallas' arm pressed against mine, our fingers intertwined. We didn't look at each other or speak, but we took strength from each other.

I couldn't bring myself to glance at Atlas or Jay.

The feeling of betrayal by Atlas was something I experienced before, right after he found out about my previous life. He'd turned his back on me and walked away. I thought that was it, we were done.

Then, I thought he'd accepted it. He'd responded by killing Bruce Fergus, the team's former GM. He explained everything and we'd moved on. I barely gave it a second thought.

But this? This was a whole other level of betrayal. We'd faked working for these people, but he hadn't. All along, he was playing us.

Where Jay stood, I didn't know. Presumably wherever Atlas did. He seemed unhappy with the situation, but he hadn't fought it. Hadn't seemed too surprised. Of course he wouldn't. Except, Atlas hadn't told him Max Stanley was alive. Unless he had and Jay faked his annoyance. That could have been another part of the act. If that was the case, he was an excellent actor. He had me fooled.

Now, we were stuck in the back of a car heading to fuck only knew where. With them.

If either of them thought they could touch me, they'd have to think again. Right now, I felt like I was held together by sticky tape and string, but when the shock was over, I'd have a few things to say to both of them. Starting with the words 'get fucked.'

"It'll be okay," Dallas whispered. "I won't let anything happen to you."

"I know you won't," I whispered back. "I won't let anything happen to you either." I hoped like hell I could keep that promise.

Jones wouldn't hesitate to kill Dallas if he got in

his way. I should have insisted he stay back with the others. Why hadn't I? Because, selfishly, I wanted him with me. I didn't want to be alone with these people, and now I might get him killed.

Am I the asshole? Yes, yes, I am.

I'd have to try to find a way to get him out of this. Maybe they'd let him walk away. He didn't have to get any deeper involved in this. He might not do it willingly, but it was for his own good. Dallas should be focusing on playing football, not being distracted by me. He should be off living his best life. He should be—

I glanced out the rear window as a flare of light blossomed in the night sky. The flames burst out above the treetops like they were trying to singe the moon.

"Bloody hell!" I gaped at the sight in absolute shock. I couldn't be seeing what I thought I was seeing. Could I? My blood turned to ice.

"Is that..." Dallas' voice wavered.

"The cottage," I said reluctantly. I tore my gaze away from the sight to glare accusingly at Jay, who sat on the other side of me, with a side eye at Atlas who sat in the front passenger seat.

They were both staring, behind us, mouths open.

Jay's face was pale. His horror looked genuine.

So did Atlas', but I knew by now how good an actor he was.

"Did you do that?" I demanded. I couldn't hold back the tears that poured down my cheeks. "You killed them."

Storm, Frost and Ramsey. And Max Stanley. If they were anywhere near the cottage, if they were inside it, they would have been incinerated. If they were lucky, they wouldn't have felt a thing. But me, I felt everything. The pieces of my broken heart shattered into a million shards. My whole beautiful world with my sexy guys was nothing more than ashes.

Atlas blinked at me a couple of times. "I did not. I had no idea." He looked ahead to the car that held Carlos Jones, then back at me. "I swear, I had nothing to do with it."

I shook my head at him in disbelief and looked away, nestling into Dallas. For a short while there, I'd almost let myself fantasise that Storm, Frost and Ramsey would come for me. They'd contact my brother and his partners and friends and find me. They'd come in, proverbial guns blazing, destroying anyone who stood in their path.

But now... It could take days for my brother to work out I was missing, much less where I'd gone. By the time he knew, I could be on the other side of the planet. I could be dead.

Or worse.

"This is bullshit," Jay whispered. "Chels, I swear I had nothing to do with this. I promise you. You saw how Atlas kept me out of the loop. I didn't even know there was a loop."

I looked over to him resentfully. "I didn't see you doing anything to stop any of this. You seemed perfectly happy to go along with it."

"I wanted to be with you and Atlas." He looked like someone kicked his basket of kittens. "That was all. I didn't want..." He glanced back out the window.

"Sure you didn't," I said sarcastically. Part of me wanted to believe him, but the rest of me was hurting too badly to throw him a lifeline. Right now, I didn't care if he and Atlas drowned.

I hated myself for loving both of them, even now. They might as well have torn my heart out and stomped all over it with footy boots. Crushed it into the grass.

Jay looked back at me, hurt in his brown eyes. "You're right, I should have stayed back with them. Then I'd be dead too." He turned away to look out the window.

I choked back a sob and turned my face to bury it

in Dallas' chest. A few hours ago, we were a perfect little family. Now, we were torn apart. Literally and figuratively. Nothing more than dust on the breeze.

"I've got you," Dallas said softly. "Whatever happens, I'm not letting you go." He stroked my hair and held me so tight I could barely breathe.

I knew he meant that. It might be the only thing I knew right now. He was the only person in the world I could trust. The only one, apart from myself, who'd get me through this. We'd get each other through this. Somehow.

"I've got you too," I managed to say. "We can do this."

What choice did we have anyway? We'd survive and find a way to get out. I'd never given up on anything yet, I wasn't going to start now. Did that mean I hadn't given up on Atlas and Jay? Deep down I wasn't ready to do that yet. We'd been through too much together already. While there was a possibility they knew nothing about blowing up the cottage, however small, I'd cling to that. It might just be the only thing that kept me sane.

We drove along the dark highway until we reached the outskirts of Dusk Bay.

Here, small houses sat on big blocks, resisting development for now. Most of them stood for close to one hundred years, while the city grew up nearby.

The driver turned the car off the highway, and up a long, winding driveway to a large house. Its grand colonial features appeared to be newly renovated and possibly extended.

Not everyone was resistant to change it, I supposed.

The car came to a stop beside Jones' vehicle. We were immediately surrounded by his armed minions. One of them opened the door beside Dallas and waved his gun to gesture for us to get out.

I wanted to tell him to fuck off. The minion, not Dallas.

Since he was armed and looked like he was willing to use the weapon, I followed Dallas out of the car, keeping physical contact with him the entire time.

Atlas and Jay came around to stand beside us.

Dallas and I both glanced at them, and deliberately kept an arm's distance between us. The moment reminded me of the days when Storm and Atlas hated each other. Maybe it would have been better if things stayed that way. Storm, Frost and Ramsey would still be alive.

Of course, I let Atlas' charms get the better of me. My pussy wanted what she wanted and now we were all fucked. I hated myself for it.

Atlas rolled his lips and looked frustrated, but he didn't say anything. He obviously got the message that I didn't want to hear it right now anyway. Nothing would excuse any of this, not now.

"Take them inside," Jones instructed.

The minion nodded. "Yes boss." He waved his gun at us again, gesturing in the direction of a side door. He walked behind us, Atlas and Jay on one side, some other minions on the other. We were outnumbered and outmuscled, so any thought of running was pushed aside for now.

Once we got inside the building, escaping would be more difficult, but we'd find a way. Dallas and I were smart and resourceful. We wouldn't stop looking for opportunities until we got our chance.

Inside, the house looked even bigger than it did from the outside. My initial perception that it was newly renovated was backed up by the large kitchen with shining appliances and dark marble countertops.

If I had to guess, I'd say the floors were original,

but the stain on them looked new. To the side of the kitchen was a sitting room with white couches and light-coloured rugs, all of which looked like they'd been put there the day before. One of the rugs was even curling upward in the corner, as if it was recently unrolled.

The whole place smelled of fresh paint.

"Welcome." Jones stretched his hands to either side. "You're my first house guests. Don't worry, we won't be here for long. I have some matters to attend to in Dusk Bay, then we'll be moving on for a while. I'm sorry I don't have time to give you a guided tour, but I'll be back in a few hours." He gave me a slick smile and a lowered his hands as though somehow I should be happy to be here.

"Take her into the room at the back," he instructed. "Keep an eye on her. I want her in one piece when I get back, ready to enjoy her."

I debated the wisdom of spitting at him, and decided it was probably not a good idea. As well as being unhygienic, he might retaliate. Getting out of here would be even more difficult if I was battered and bruised.

No, I'd restrain myself. For now.

"We'll see she stays put," Atlas said. "She can be a handful, but we know how to handle her."

I raised an eyebrow at him. I wanted to handle his cock with my knee, or maybe a brick. I forced myself not to think about his cock. That kind of thinking would only lead to increased frustration and anger at his betrayal. I'd let him fuck me and this was how he responded? That was in no way okay with me.

Dallas squeezed my hand tight. So tight, I could tell what he was thinking. He was trying not to snap at Atlas, or anyone else here. He wanted to tell them to keep their hands off me. But he knew speaking out could get him killed. If he was dead, he couldn't be with me anymore. We'd already seen what they'd done to my other three boyfriends. I couldn't lose him too.

I had to give him credit for his self control. Storm would have told them to ram it up their ass.

I swallowed down a heavy ball of grief and let them lead me to a back room as the weight of everything that happened tonight started to settle on my shoulders.

Chapter Eight

Chelsea

Atlas and Jay followed us in before the door was closed and locked behind us.

"What the hell?" Dallas finally found his voice. "I should fuck both of you up."

His face was almost white with fury he'd kept suppressed until now. He took half a step away from me and stood facing them, hands in fists in front of him.

Atlas scoffed. "You killed one person in self-defence and we found you, curled up in a ball on the floor, remember?"

"I was not curled up in a fucking ball," Dallas snarled. "I was slowly processing it. I won't need to take that time with either of you."

Jay held his hands up in front of himself. "Bro,

we didn't do anything." He glanced sidelong at Atlas before correcting himself. "*I* didn't do anything."

Atlas frowned at him, but it was Dallas who spoke first.

"Don't call me bro, asshole. You turned your back on Chelsea. On all of us. You pretended you gave a shit about us and you were working for that prick the entire time." He gestured vaguely towards the door.

"I wasn't," Jay said in a small voice.

All of our eyes turned to Atlas.

He looked back at us. One eyebrow twitched. He scratched his ear. Glanced at the wall. Looked back at us.

"You don't have anything to say for yourself?" Dallas demanded. A moment later, what Atlas was trying to convey sank in.

The walls have ears. Of course, someone would be listening to everything we were saying. What did that mean though?

Was he really on our side? I wanted to believe he was. Desperately.

"It's been a long night," Atlas said finally. "Why don't we all get some rest?"

I didn't want to turn my back on him, so I half-turned and took in the rest of the room.

A large bed sat in the middle, between two

windows. Under one was our bags, which must have been brought in ahead of us.

To the side of the room was a door that led into a bathroom.

Like the kitchen and living area, everything here was light in colour and looked new. The duvet cover on the bed even had creases where it had been removed from a box and placed on the bed. The pillowcases had the same creases.

"At least it's clean," Jay said.

"As prisons go, I've seen worse," I said.

None of us were chained to the wall. Yet.

"Get some rest," Atlas said again. "I'll keep watch."

Was he saying that because he wanted to watch out for us, or because he knew none of us wanted to lie next to him right now? Did I really give a shit?

I was starting to think I could still trust Jay. The three of us were more than a match for Atlas if we decided to deal with him ourselves. Although it would take one shout from him to call the minions into the room, so it would do us little good to try.

Just in case, I checked the windows. Both were locked and the panes too small to crawl through, even if we broke the glass.

With a sigh, because I knew I'd get nowhere

without any rest, I kicked off my shoes and lay down on the side of the bed. Dallas gave Jay a long look before lying down in the middle, keeping himself between us. He put his arm over me and held me to him. For once, making no move to fuck me.

Shame. I wouldn't have minded messing up these clean sheets. After the long day and exhausting night, I was tired.

In spite of that, I didn't know if I was going to be able to sleep in this place. All I could think of were Storm, Frost and Ramsey. Had they felt anything when the cottage exploded? Did they know they were about to die? Did they feel much pain or none at all?

There were times when being a doctor sucked. This was one of them. I had way too much knowledge of the impact of an explosion on human bodies. What they would have felt and where. Unless it was instant. All I could do was hope it was quick and they didn't suffer. They deserved nothing less. They were good men who should have had another sixty years ahead of them at least. We should have grown old together, until we were all grey and wrinkled. Now, none of them would get old. The team was going to fall apart without them. Hell, I was going to fall apart without them. Not now, because I had to hold it all together. But when this was over, I'd let myself grieve for as long as it took. Probably forever. I'd never get over loving and losing the three of them. Each of them would always hold a piece of my heart.

I could almost hear Storm saying, "Fucking right, you're mine even if I'm dead. You'll always belong to me."

A tear slid down my cheek. It didn't seem real that they were gone. I wished I was in the middle of a nightmare and soon would wake up. I'd find myself lying in bed, in our mansion, my guys around me. Frost snoring and Storm muttering in his sleep. That was a better reality than this. One minute we were standing there, ready to defend ourselves, and now...

"This is fucked up," Dallas whispered. His voice was choked with emotion.

All I could manage in reply was a soft, "Yeah."

Fucked up was one way to put it. Screwed up, heartbreaking, devastating, confusing...

I felt very small lying there on sheets that smelled of cardboard and plastic.

Frost would have complained that they could have washed the sheets before putting them on the bed. Storm would have given him a funny look and told him to be quiet and go to sleep.

And Ramsey, he would have wanted to go and do

a workout. To burn off his frustration. I never did get around to sitting down with him and talking about that. I should have taken the time. Now I'd never get the opportunity to. What else had I missed out on doing?

So many things, including growing old with all of them. Maybe having children some day. I'd never get to experience any of that with them. I'd never get to hear their voices or feel their touch.

"Maybe they got out in time," Jay suggested in a small voice.

"Don't," I said.

"I was just—" he started.

"Getting my hopes up for nothing," I said. "I don't want to start thinking they might walk through the door when they won't."

I couldn't even let myself consider the possibility they might be alive. That would only lead to more heartbreak when it was inevitably confirmed. They were gone.

I usually didn't think of myself as a pessimist, but right now I was. How else could I possibly be? My heart was too heavy. As it was, I was barely keeping myself from sobbing.

If I started, I wouldn't stop. And Jones would

win. There was no way in hell I was letting him do that. No matter what, he didn't get to win.

I was going to find a way out of here and I was going to destroy him.

Never before in my life had I felt the part of mafia princess. That was the person I hadn't let myself be. I ran from it for my entire life. Hid from it like it might go away if I ignored it.

But now I knew, all along I'd been hiding from a piece of myself. A huge piece I couldn't deny any longer. It was as much a part of me as breathing. Daze was right, this was who I was. That admission to myself made me breathless for a few moments. It felt as though all the pieces of the puzzle fell into place and clicked. Nothing in my life made more sense than this. Nothing.

I was finally ready to embrace who I was.

More than embrace it. I was ready to burn the whole fucking world down.

If he thought he could kill my men and get away with it, he'd think twice when I was done with him. He'd wish he was chained up in Ice's workroom. He'd beg to have the skin peeled off him section by section. He'd plead to have his fingers and toes removed with a plier. He'd scream and ask to die.

What I was going to do to him, it would be a

thousand times worse. It might involve an anthill and honey, I didn't know.

Whatever it was, his life would be a living hell, just like he was determined my life would become. Now more than ever, I had to be strong. I had to be the badass woman people kept telling me I could be. I had to be all of that and more. When I was done, they wouldn't even find Jones' ashes.

If my brother was here right now, he'd be impressed. Angry, but impressed.

"I'm sorry," Jay said after a couple of minutes of silence. "I didn't mean to..."

"I know," I said. "Get some rest. We're going to need it to get out of this shit."

"You really think we can?" Dallas asked.

"What kind of question is that?" I asked, more harshly than I intended. "Of course we can, and we will. We've been through a lot and we survived, we can get through this."

My heart was still heavy, but it started to feel stony as well. Like it was locking away deep inside my chest to protect me from any further pain. Placed inside a lead box no one could open.

Good, I needed to be harder than steel. I couldn't let anyone in anymore. I wouldn't let anyone break me.

Let them fucking try.

"You're right," he said. "We've got this." He didn't sound as certain as I would have liked him to, but he'd also dragged himself together. I hoped like hell he could stay together. If he fell apart, I might as well. And I wasn't sure if I had enough strength for both of us.

What was I saying? If he fell apart, I'd have no choice but to toughen up even more. And I would. Because that was what badass mafia princesses did. We raised hell and we took names. We destroyed our enemies and left them in pieces, broken on the floor. We tore them to shreds and feasted on the scraps.

When I was finished, Daze and Mina would be looking up to me. Hell, maybe I'd be the one to take Reuben Brantley's place. If he couldn't keep the Crimson Vipers in line, maybe Dusk Bay needed someone who could.

Doctor Chelsea Miller was done being a fucking doormat for assholes. This was what they wanted me to become, they could deal with the consequences. I didn't care if I left the world in ruins behind me.

The people who killed my men were going to pay and they were going to pay dearly.

Chapter Nine

Chelsea

I woke a few hours later with Dallas' hand between my legs.

He was only grazing his fingers lightly up and down the inside of my thigh and over the gusset of my panties, but it was enough to get me going. Even with us being where we currently were. Even with me being uncertain he was actually awake.

Still, I parted my legs wider to give him better access. When he hooked his finger into the side of my panties and pulled them aside, I decided he must be awake after all.

Was it crazy to be turned on in this place? Probably. Did I give a shit? A small one. We were locked in here and Jones' minions could walk in at any moment. Jones himself could. Three of my guys were dead and at least one was dubiously trustworthy.

Yet, this was my life and I wasn't going to let anyone stop me from living it. Badass women did what they wanted, when they wanted. Right?

Of course we did.

I peeked out over the covers to see Atlas sitting against the wall near the door. His head was down, chin to his chest. He seemed to be asleep. On the other side of Dallas, so was Jay. I thought about waking him, so the three of us could deal with Atlas while he slept, but even as I pondered, Atlas stirred.

The fact he was locked in here with us at all suggested Jones didn't trust him either. What did that mean? I decided to let myself go for a few minutes and think about it later. That was an issue for post-orgasm me.

"You're so wet," Dallas whispered. His fingers went still. "I'm sorry, I shouldn't be..."

"Don't stop," I told him. "I need this right now and so do you. I want this."

"Are you sure?" He moved his fingers again, running up and down my seam and dipping into my damp entrance.

"Completely," I said firmly. As stress relievers went, sex was one of the best, if not *the* best. Otis

Skinner banged on about water therapy, but I preferred, well, bang therapy. Maybe I should have become a sex therapist instead of practising sports medicine. If I was an expert on anything, it was fucking.

"I love you," he whispered. "If I was going to get stuck in a beige house like this, locked in with anyone, I'm glad it's you."

"Why do I get the impression you're more offended by beige then you are being locked in?" I teased gently.

"Just trying to... lighten the mood," he said.

For a moment there, I was sure he was going to say he was trying to channel Frost. If anyone was going to crack jokes right now, it would be... Would have been, him. We needed humour right now. Humour and orgasms.

"The decor is boring," I said finally. "For someone like Jones, I would have expected bright orange everywhere."

Dallas snorted and slipped a finger inside me. "I guess even evil assholes have their limit."

"Who would have thought?" I bent my knees to spread my legs wider, encouraging him to put it another finger inside me, then another.

"What are we thinking?" Jay asked, with a yawn.

He appeared over Dallas' shoulder. His eyes widened seeing what we were doing. "Oh, I see." He glanced over toward Atlas. "There might be a camera."

"I don't care," I said. "Let them watch." In spite of that, I reached down under the covers to slide the heel of my hand up and down the front of Dallas' pants. He was already hard, but became harder still under my touch.

"I'll keep guard." Jay sat up, his arms crossed over his chest.

I exchanged glances with Dallas and shook my head slightly. I wanted to believe Jay was on our side, but would I bank on it? Not yet.

His feelings for me seemed to be genuine, but he'd been with Atlas a lot longer than he knew the rest of us. If push came to shove, where would his loyalty be? I wasn't sure he even knew.

Dallas started to pump his hand in and out of me, pushing the majority of the coherent thought to the side. I let it go and rocked my hips against his hand, making his fingers as wet as my pussy.

"I love the sounds you make when when I'm touching you," he whispered. "You're always so responsive. So gorgeous. Thank you for being mine."

"Thank you for knowing just the right way to

touch me," I whispered back. He always knew just the right places and pressure. Never too much and never too little. Everything he did, he always watched me for my reaction, giving me more when I liked it and changing if it wasn't quite right. I'd never known anyone so attentive to my needs.

"I try." He hooked his fingers around and wrapped me from the inside while moving the heel of his hand up and down my clit.

In turn, I worked my hand under the front of his track pants and gripped his cock. He was so hard, thick and throbbing. So ready.

"You have magic hands," he told me.

I stroked my fingers up and down him. "I was going to say the same to you." He had me so close already. Even in this place, he got me going like crazy.

"Let's call it a draw," he said. He rolled his hips, pushing himself into my hand, the head of his cock nudging my palm.

"Deal," I said. I glanced past him to see Jay watching us. The moment I locked my eyes on his, he looked away.

"I'm watching the door," he said quickly.

"I don't mind if you watch us," I said.

He wouldn't be able to do more than give us a

quick warning anyway. What would we do then? Probably keep doing exactly what we were doing.

"I'm watching the door," Atlas said. He must have woken in the last few minutes. I got the impression he knew what was going on, and he wasn't going to try to stop us either. Good, because I would have ignored him. He liked to be in charge, but not of this. This was happening whether he wanted it to or not.

I looked back to Dallas, who shrugged and went on working me with his expert fingers. I decided to forget about Atlas and everything else for a while and lose myself here, with his touch.

"Can you come for me?" Dallas asked. He almost seemed to be pleading. Like somehow he wasn't doing his job right if I couldn't come here.

"I can and I will," I said. I half-closed my eyes, keeping them on his face while I let myself go. Letting him drive me closer and closer and over the edge. I bit my lip to keep from crying out.

Not because I cared about being overheard, but because I wasn't going to let any of Jones' minions have the pleasure of hearing me come. Especially Jones himself. That was something he'd never get from me, not from watching via a camera and definitely not in person.

I rocked my hips harder, letting the orgasm last

for as long as I could before I finally came back down to earth.

"Can I..." Dallas looked tentative, his fingers still deep inside me.

"I want you to," I told him. His fingers were lovely, but I needed to feel his cock inside me. My body, heart and soul needed it. Okay, the part of me which was rebelling against being locked in here needed it too. The part of me that was not going to roll over like a lapdog and let Jones rub my belly. I'd sooner bite his hand off.

Although, I wanted no part of him anywhere near my mouth. Or any other part of me for that matter.

Visibly relieved, he slid his fingers out, pressed them to my lips and held them there while I sucked them clean. He watched avidly, as though it was his cock in my mouth. I sucked extra hard, pretending it was, knowing it was getting him going more.

"I taste good," I said.

He leaned over to kiss my mouth before pulling the covers over us and kneeling between my knees. He pushed himself inside me with uncharacteristically slow movements, easing inside rather than slamming desperately. He exhaled slowly out his nose before thrusting, just as slow. Sliding all the way in and pulling all the way back out again. Every movement deliberate and careful.

"I feel like I've always rushed with you," he whispered into my ear. "Because when I'm inside you, I can't think of anything else. All I want to do is fuck you until I come, then fuck you again. But I don't want to rush anymore. I want to enjoy you, to feel you. Really feel you. I'm sorry if I was in too much of a hurry." He shook his head, his brow creased.

"I never felt like you were in a hurry," I told him. "I'm flattered I turn you on so much."

There was no right way to fuck, only different ways. As long as you were attentive to the needs of your partner, and yourself, then anything goes. He never made me feel neglected or unappreciated. Exactly the opposite. I liked his enthusiasm. My pussy liked the attention; it was good for my ego. What girl doesn't want to feel wanted by someone she loves, whether it be sexual or emotional? In his case, it was both and I was here for it.

"You do." He thrust slightly faster a couple of times before slowing himself back down again. "I'm sorry," he said again."

I cupped his cheek with my hand. "Never be sorry for being you. I wouldn't want you any other way. You're perfect just as you are, okay?" I raised my eyebrows at him, letting him know I meant what I said and wanted him to not only listen but agree. He was a wonderful guy. I needed him to know that. I wanted him to see himself the way I saw him. As a guy who was more than worthy of my love and affection. Deserving of touching and being touched, embraced, held. Loved.

He managed a smile before giving in to the need to pound more rapidly. Much more like himself. He let out a long breath, like he'd held it in when he held himself back. Now, he gave me everything, driving into me over and over until he went still and came inside me.

As if him letting go triggered something in me, I came again, harder than before, once again pressing my lips together to hold in the sound. My pussy tightened around Dallas' cock, as if we might lock together forever. For those few moments, we were all but fused, two people become one.

Gradually, my muscles relaxed, letting him go again. For now.

"You're so incredible," he said breathlessly. "So amazing."

"No, you," I told him. I caught Jay's eye again. He looked uncomfortable, like he hated to be on the outer with us. Like he was trying to figure out what he could say that would make everything right. He glanced towards Atlas and sagged slightly.

Yeah, nothing was going to be that simple. At least not for a while.

I lay back, my heart gradually slowing, catching my breath.

In the corner of my consciousness, I was aware of movement outside the room. Footsteps and voices drawing closer.

A couple of moments later, the door was unlocked with a click and pushed open.

Chapter Ten

Chelsea

I EXPECTED TO SEE JONES WITH A MINION OR two in tow, but it wasn't him who walked through the door.

Instead, a woman stepped into the room. Around my age, maybe a handful of years older, her hair was cut short to frame her face. Her septum was pierced with a simple silver ring. Rows of matching sleepers decorated her earlobes.

She stalked towards us, the thighs of her leather pants making a swishing sound as she walked.

"I see you're awake," she said smoothly. The soles of her tall boots clicked on the floor as she walked toward the bed.

Atlas was on his feet now, watching her carefully.

"What an astute observation," I said sarcastically. I sat up, keeping the sheets over my breasts. I didn't give a shit if she knew what we were just doing, but I wasn't giving her an eyeful either.

She smiled, but the look in her eyes was shrewd and dangerous. "I'm known for my astute observations, Doctor Miller. And my ability to get what I want."

"What do you want?" Atlas stayed near the door, watching the couple of minions who'd entered the room behind her.

She ignored him. "I suggest you fix your clothes. Carlos will be here soon to have you all moved to another location. He told you about that, didn't he?" She didn't seem to care either way. "If you think he'll wait for you, you better think again. He won't hesitate to haul you all out naked in front of everyone." For some reason, that seemed to irritate her.

"I'm sure he wouldn't," I said.

"He better fucking not," Dallas growled. "He'll have to go past us."

She snorted derisively. "Sweetie, he'll just kill you if you get in his way."

I bristled at the threat. Not to mention her calling him sweetie. "If he wants my cooperation, he better not touch a hair on any of their heads."

"It's not your cooperation he wants," she said. "He doesn't care about that. He has other people to cooperate with him."

"Then he can let us go," I said, pretending I didn't understand exactly what she was referring to. Both of us knew exactly what she was saying. Jones would take me, whether I was willing or if it was by force. Men like him didn't stop to ask permission. Or forgiveness.

"You know he won't do that until he's done with you," she said. "If he ever is. Let me tell you a few things." She grabbed a chair from the side of the room and pulled it over to sit in front of us. She twisted around to nod at the minions. "You can go."

One of them opened his mouth to answer, but she stared them down until they backed out the door and closed it behind them.

"You're very sure we won't kill you now you're alone in here with us," Atlas remarked. He stepped around the chair to stand beside her. His arms were by his sides, but his hands curling and uncurling as if he was ready to wrap them around her throat and squeeze. None of us would stop him.

"You won't do that," she said, barely looking at him. "You know if you do, you'll be next. And we're supposed to be on the same side, remember?" Now she looked up at him and gave him the same dangerous smile.

"Maybe I'll kill you," I said to her. "I'm not on the same side as him." I gave him a glare Storm would have been proud of. I wished he was here to do it himself. He would have done a more convincing job of threatening her.

"Then he'd have to stop you." She jerked her head towards Atlas. "And if he didn't, how would that look?"

"What do you want?" I was done with her bullshit. If she'd come here to say something, she might as well go ahead and say it.

"Do you know who I am?" she asked.

I almost said I didn't, but realised I knew exactly who she was the moment she stepped into the room. "Nyla Fox. Carlos Jones' right hand."

"I prefer the term 'successor,'" she said.

"Can you take over from him today?" Jay asked. "Because he'd be dead then," he added, in case anyone missed his meaning.

"Works for me," Dallas muttered.

I would have agreed, but I had the impression she was more dangerous than Jones. Although, she probably didn't have a cock, so that was a bonus.

Unless she decided the guys should please her. In which case, I *would* kill her.

"Are you suggesting there might be some kind of conflict between Carlos and me?" One of her perfectly shaped eyebrows twitched upward, a piercing there glittering in the overhead light.

"Carlos Jones is an asshole," I said bluntly. "There's conflict between him and me. There's going to be a shit load of conflict between him and my family when they come looking for me. If there isn't any between you and him, then you can look forward to a slow, painful death alongside him." It wasn't even an empty threat. That was exactly what would happen. All of us held grudges and had long memories.

Nyla smiled. "You're everything I expected you to be. Finally."

I frowned at her. "What are you talking about?" She couldn't possibly be implying what I thought she was, could she?

She leaned forward and placed her hands on her knees. Her nails were long, painted matte black. "You and your friend getting shot at. How is she doing, by the way?"

"Fine." That was all she was getting from me. She didn't deserve to know anything more about Sadie.

The fact she knew my friend existed was bad enough.

"I'm so glad," she said, clearly not giving too many shits either way. "Then there was India, and Sierra. Such a shame to lose both of them, but it was what it was."

Beside me, Dallas stiffened at the mention of India's name. Did Nyla know he had anything to do with that? Judging by the way her eyes slid to him and back again, she did. Jones must have told her after Atlas told him. At this point, we might as well have written it in the sky. It seemed she wasn't going to retaliate. Not yet at least.

"Is there a point to all of this?" Atlas demanded. "Maybe you could get to it. Like you said, they should fix their clothes before Jones gets here."

She glanced at him dismissively before her intense gaze was back on me. "You don't get it, do you? There was a reason behind everything that happened. Remember Belinda Simmons? Did you ever wonder how she found out you used to be a stripper? Did you wonder how Dominic King knew? How the press found out yesterday? Did it occur to you that people being shot, or shot at in your vicinity, might not be coincidental?"

"Of course I have," I said sharply. "Belinda just

did some digging around. She spoke to some people—"

Nyla laughed. "She wished she was that intelligent and capable. No, she was tipped off."

"By you?" Atlas asked.

"People who work for me, yes," she said. "Because I told them to. They encouraged her to look into you and ask you questions. She was only too happy to."

"Why?" I frowned at her. "Why would you bother?" What was I missing here? I didn't even know this woman. Why would she go to so much effort to insinuate herself into my life?

"Because it was fun," she said. "And because I knew what you'd do. Belinda Simmons was getting too close to a couple of things I didn't want her near. I needed her taken care of."

"Why not get someone else to do it?" Atlas asked. "Why involve Chelsea?"

"Because I know who she is," Nyla said, without taking her eyes off me. "Who she really is. I know she's been in denial for a long time and that's frustrated some people."

"Boo fucking hoo," I said sarcastically. Okay, I *was* finally ready to embrace that side of myself, but was she really saying she pushed me to it? That she engineered everything which happened to us just so

I'd step back out of my comfort zone and into the crazy lifestyle I'd worked so hard to stay out of? All of the blood, sweat and tears were because of her? Why?

I stiffened my back and raised my chin proudly. I outranked her and we both knew it. She didn't get to push me around.

In theory.

"I get to decide who and what I am."

She laughed. "If I had a dollar for every time someone told me that, I'd be richer than I already am. I've been pulling your strings from the start and you've been dancing on them like a good girl."

How far would I get if I launched myself at her and wrapped my hands around her throat? The guys wouldn't stop me. At least, Dallas and Jay wouldn't. I wasn't so sure about Atlas.

"You killed my boyfriends," I said, my voice stony cold.

Her expression became serious. "That wasn't me. That was all Carlos. Which brings me to my point."

"It's about time," Atlas said under his breath.

"I was aware of his attraction to you," she said slowly.

"Jealous?" I asked.

She snort-laughed. "Hardly. Him killing your

boyfriends helped me, in a way. It should make this easier for me." Her eyes were stone cold. Talking about three men dying didn't even reach her. She might have been talking about what she ate for dinner the night before. Of course, people like her were familiar with death. So much so it didn't matter. As long as it wasn't them, then they didn't care.

Until yesterday, I would have been horrified. But now I was starting to understand how anyone could become like that. At some point, you had to switch off or it would destroy you from the inside out. And yet, she was still talking about my guys.

They weren't nothing. They were everything. They deserved better than to be a footnote in the conversation. So much better.

There was that urge to strangle her again. I curled my hands around the top of the sheets and struggled to push the grief aside. I couldn't lose it, not in front of her. Not in front of anyone. I was done being vulnerable. I had to be made of steel. Stronger and tougher than I'd ever been. Able to bend but not break. Nothing else would get me through this. These next few hours and the rest of my life.

"How could them dying help you?" I asked. My tone was tighter than the top of the drum. So tight if I touched it, it might snap. Rage barely contained.

Ready to grab a drum of oil and light a match to set everything on fire. Right now, I didn't care who got burnt. If they got in my way, they'd be incinerated.

Don't lose your shit, I told myself. *That's what they want. If you do that, they win.*

I was not letting them win. My guys didn't die for nothing. Their deaths meant others would suffer, would pay for taking them from me. I'd see to that if it was the last thing I did.

Nyla leaned even further forward. When she spoke, it was barely a whisper, only loud enough for us to hear.

"Them dying changed everything, you have to admit that. Because it made you angry. Angrier than anything I could have done to you. I need you angry. Because you're Carlos' weakness. Together, we can bring him down."

Chapter Eleven

Ramsey

"Well that's fucked," Frost remarked.

He stood beside the SUV, arms crossed over his chest, surveying what was left of his cottage. "I was fond of that place too."

"It could have been worse." Storm matched his pose. "We could have been inside."

Frost nodded. "Yes we could. That would have been much more fucked."

"We got lucky," I said. "If we were any closer to that, it would have taken us out."

I leaned against the side of the SUV, away from the still roaring blaze. It was already starting to die down, and so far hadn't spread beyond the cottage. We were also lucky it wasn't the middle of summer, because if the area was dry, it would ignite like the perfect kindling. The whole forest would go up so fast we'd be lucky to get out in time.

"I would have been pissed off if that happened," Frost said. "I'd haunt Jones for the rest of his life."

"Ghosts aren't real," Storm said.

"They would be if I died. Otherwise I wouldn't be able to throw things at him and scare the shit out of him." Frost said with a shrug. "We should go."

"Yeah, we should," I agreed. "Sooner or later, they'll come back to check if they finished us off or not."

"I'm starting to take this personally," Max said, his expression grim.

"Funny, I was thinking the same thing." Frost opened the front passenger door and climbed inside. "I think they wanted all of us dead."

"It's going to take a lot more than an explosive device to kill me," Storm declared.

If he was inside the cottage, he'd be very much dead, but I didn't bother to correct him. There was nothing wrong with being relieved at not being blown to kingdom come.

We got lucky, and luckier still the SUV was in one piece. The side closest to the cottage was dented from a couple of boards that struck there, thrown by the force of the blast. Other than that, it survived.

Just as well. I wouldn't have minded the jog to the highway, but it would have taken up too much precious time. So would calling someone to come and get us.

I slid into the back beside Max and pulled out my phone to send off a couple of messages. I didn't need to see Ice's expression to know how pissed off he was going to be when he read the one I sent him.

Storm half turned to look back at me. "Where are we going? We don't know where they've taken her. Unless they got a flat tyre, they'll be long gone by the time we reach the highway."

He seethed with anger and regret. So did I, but I kept myself tightly under control. Losing our shit wouldn't help Chelsea. We needed to be calmer and more focused now than when we were on the rugby field. So much more was at stake.

Before I could answer, a message popped up on my phone.

I glanced down at the screen. Ice responded with an address. That was all. No rants, no angry face emojis. No mention of what he'd to to Carlos Jones, or Atlas and Jay.

In spite of that, I could almost feel his fury from here. Between us, we were going to destroy anyone who dared to lay a hand on Chelsea.

"Where *are* we going?" Max asked. He looked as though he'd prefer to be anywhere but here. To be honest, so would I.

"*We're* going," I corrected. "We'll drop *you* off somewhere. You've been involved enough. I know a place. You'll be safe until we deal with this."

He looked like he wanted to argue, but finally nodded. "Right. I think that's a good idea. Whatever this is, it's..." He swallowed visibly.

"It's bullshit, is what it is," Storm said. "You shouldn't have been involved in the first fucking place. We should have killed King and Skinner before everything went too far. None of us would be here now if we had."

"No, you'd probably be dead," I agreed.

Max shifted in his seat, clearly uncomfortable at this topic of conversation.

I had to respect a man who could admit when he was in over his head. He was definitely in over his. He was a football coach, not a mobster. Not for now at least. What happened after this— That was up to him. Once the shock was over, he might decide he was in it for the adrenaline, or to protect the team. Stranger things had happened.

"Drive out to the highway," I said to Storm. "There's a road about two kilometres down. We'll leave Coach there before we keep going."

"Can we trust him to keep his mouth closed?" Frost looked back at him, as though he'd offer to kill him if necessary.

Max raised his hands. "No one will hear the word about this from me. Who'd believe it anyway?"

"You'd be surprised," I said dryly. "You won't have to say anything to anyone. My aunt Clarissa will make sure of that. No one will find you there with her."

"Are you sure of that?" Frost asked.

"One hundred percent," I said. "There's nowhere safer in Dusk Bay than Aunt Clarissa's." No one could get in, and Max couldn't get out. She'd see to it. She'd been a certified badass since before I was born. She also managed to keep such a low profile most people didn't even know she existed. I grew up wanting to be like her, but football got me first.

We drove in silence for a few minutes before I directed Storm to turn down a side road.

The 'road' looked like nothing more than a forestry track, which was the point. In reality, it was private property, so forestry workers didn't come here. The public didn't either. A 'no through road' sign made sure of that.

Not to mention a gate that only opened with a code I sent from my phone. The gate itself was the kind forestry placed on tracks where they didn't want people driving. Heavy forest to either side prevented anyone from going around it. The whole setup was subtle but effective. Exactly what you'd expect from a forest track. A huge iron gate would raise too much suspicion.

That came another kilometre down the track, before we reached a small house nestled in the forest.

"Nice shack," Storm remarked, clearly unimpressed.

"Don't let the outside fool you." I pushed out the door and jerked my head to the side to indicate that Max should follow.

The other three were right behind me as I approached the front of the house.

The door swung open. Aunt Clarissa greeted us with a warm smile. Almost as tall as me, she was broad everywhere, including her shoulders. She had that look about her, like she could take all three of us out with a single punch and gone back inside to finish a cup of tea.

"Ferris! What are you doing here?" She enveloped me in a hug so tight I struggled to breathe.

"Just leaving our coach with you for safekeeping." I managed to survive the hug, barely, and stepped back to indicate Max.

She looked him up and down. "Nice. It's been a while since I've had company out here."

He was actually blushing while I explained the situation in as few words as possible.

Her smile faded and was replaced with anger on our behalf.

"What can I do?" She placed her hands on her wide hips. "I haven't been to town much since I sold my vegan grocery store, but I still know people."

That was an understatement and we both knew it. She regularly ate dinner with Daisy Lasalle and Mina DiMarco. She was as tight with them as anyone could be.

"Just keep Coach safe," I told her. "We'll be back for him." I knew she'd arm herself and ride with us if necessary, but we needed her here. When the dust finally settled, the team would need its head coach back. He couldn't be in better hands here. If I wasn't mistaken, he didn't mind a bit.

"No offence, but this place doesn't look very

secure." Storm stood with his head tilted, frowning at the shack, as he referred to it.

"None taken," Clarissa said dryly. "That's the idea. This part looks like nothing special. The three stories underground are something else." She smiled at his surprise. "Gets 'em every time. Next time Ferris brings you by, I might show you around."

Storm didn't look like he quite believed her, but he shrugged and straightened his head. "Sure, I'd be down for that. After we get Chelsea away from that asshole."

"If you need anything, you know where to find me." Clarissa beckoned Max to step inside and gave me another hug before she followed him in and closed the door.

"Fifty bucks says they get together by the end of the month," Frost said.

"Hundred bucks says end of the week." Storm jangled his keys in his hand as we headed back to the SUV.

They both looked at me. I shrugged. "I don't want to think about my aunt's sex life. Except to say, he could do a lot worse than her."

She'd been alone for a long time. She deserved to have someone looking out for her. So did Coach Stanley. He was a good man. They'd be nice together. But that wasn't my concern at that moment. All I could think about was getting to Chelsea and hoping like hell we were there in time.

I gave Storm the address, climbed back into the SUV and sat with my hands by my side, feeling every second tick by.

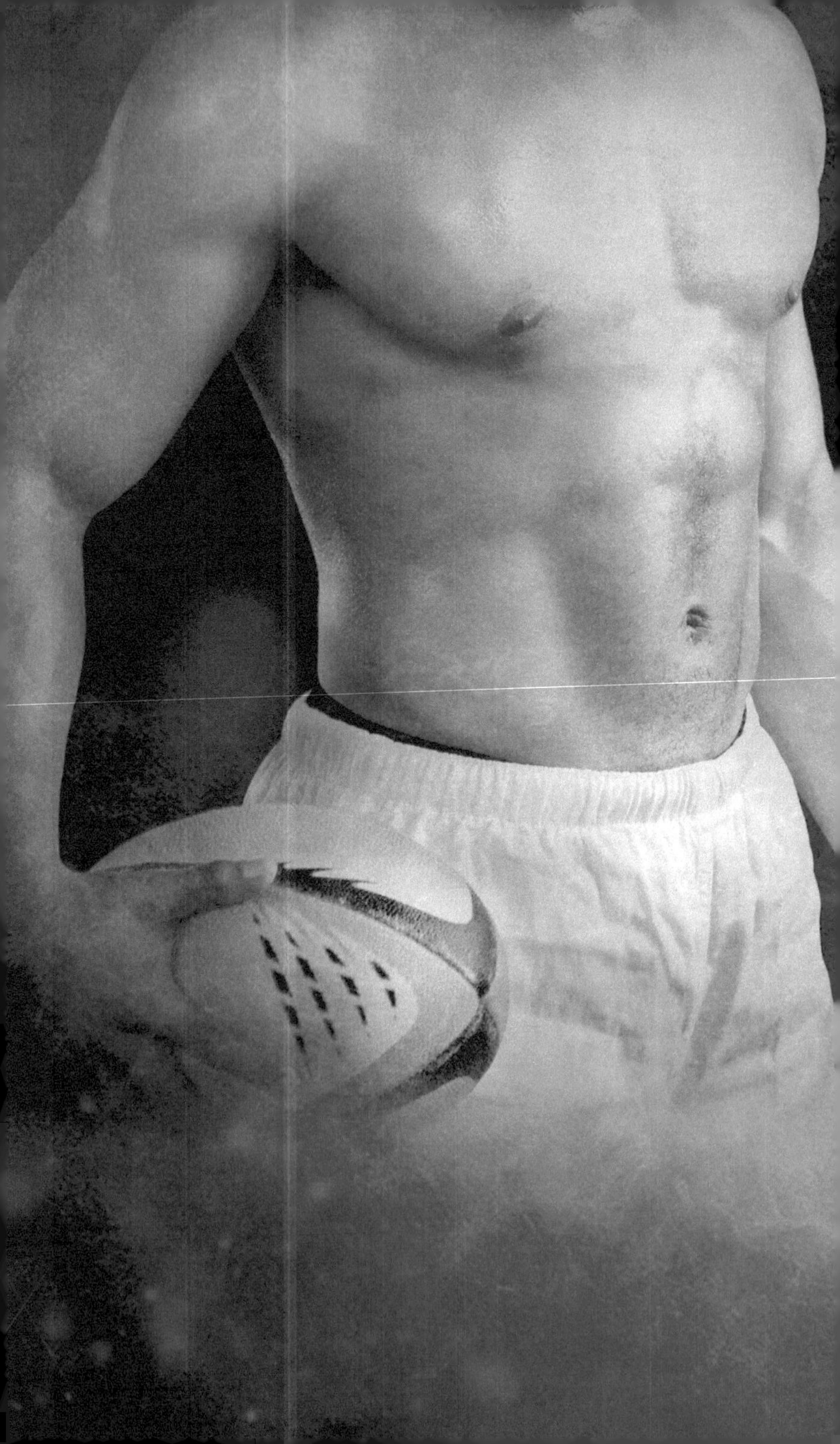

Chapter Twelve

Chelsea

"WHY WOULD WE HELP YOU?" I ASKED, LOOKING Nyla Fox straight in the eyes.

I barely flinched when she said she wanted to take down Carlos Jones. Either she was sincere, or she was bullshitting. Either way, we were still locked in here. My priority was getting out, not playing by her tune. Not unless it suited me and my guys. Then I might consider it.

"Why should we believe a word you say?" Jay asked. "This could be some kind of setup." He glanced around the room, looking for cameras or microphones.

Nyla rolled her eyes. "I come in here suggesting you help me take down Carlos, and you think I'm setting you up? Think about that for a moment. If anyone is listening to us, who are they going to point fingers at? You, for lying there and being sceptical, or me? The one who stepped into the room, sent everyone else away and laid my cards on the proverbial table? How do you think that would go down if Carlos knew?"

"If you're putting yourself at risk, can you be sure he can't hear?" I asked.

This could be nothing more than some sick, twisted game. Pretend she was on our side before she screwed us over. Maybe she was bored and needed something to do. Why not fuck with us? People did less for shits and giggles.

"I can be absolutely certain," she said without flinching. "I was the one who found this place and set it up. I know how to turn the cameras and microphones on and off. In fact, they're all connected to my phone." She tapped a pocket in her thigh, and the rectangular shape under the leather. "No one can turn them back on except for me."

"Unless they kill you and take your phone," Atlas said.

She shrugged. "Unless that. But they wouldn't know to do that, because he thinks I'm a good little general. In actual fact, I've been working for quite some time to bring him down. You just happened to be the perfect tool to help me do that." For a moment, she seemed sincere. The bravado an act she set aside and showed the real her underneath. A hint of vulnerability amongst women.

"Why do you want to bring him down?" I asked.

Did I believe her? Not really, but I might as well humour her. For now, anyway. It wasn't like I had anything better to do. Okay, I had about a million things better than this to do, but while we were locked in I was out of choices. But I was still looking for a chance to get the hell out of here. It might come from her if I paid close enough attention.

"Because he had my parents killed," she said. "They stood in his way. He wanted me and my sisters to belong to the cartel. In every sense of the word."

Her expression darkened that hint of vulnerability laid bare. In a way, she reminded me of myself. I had to shove that thought away, it was dangerous. Finding things in common with this woman made me the vulnerable one. I reminded myself she was the enemy here, not my new best friend.

Eyes hard again, she went on. "I pretended to be a dutiful woman. I managed to get his trust and work my way up through the ranks. Stepping on anyone and everyone that had a part in my parents' murder as I went."

Now that I believed. Chances were, she had more blood on her hands than me and my brother did. Those boots of hers had likely indented so many skulls she'd lost count. Stepping on people was what the cartel did. They didn't care who, as long as they got what they wanted. She was no different.

She toyed with one of the rings on her ear. "Carlos Jones is the last of them. But he's also the most difficult. He's always surrounded by other people. Oh, I could shoot him in the head, but then I'd be killed too. No, I need to separate him from them, and find a way they can't retaliate until I take over." Her eyes were glazed, clearly thinking about her plans, and relishing the idea of his death.

That made two of us. I was looking forward to seeing him dead too. I should be alarmed at how fast I was losing myself, but then I thought about Storm, Frost and Ramsey, and I was furious all over again.

"Who's to say you wouldn't be worse than him?" I asked coldly.

She smiled. "I might be, but I wouldn't be as bad to you as he would. Or to any other women. The Crimson Vipers have always been led by a man. An old one. That needs to stop. It's time for someone younger to step up and lead the cartel. Someone who doesn't need to exploit vulnerable people in order to feel good."

"Why you?" I asked. "Why not me?"

For the first time, she looked surprised. She didn't laugh, as I might have expected her to. Instead, she looked thoughtful.

"I'm not going to let you take this from me, but that's not to say we can't work together. You have the connections and the background. We'd be one hell of a team."

"What if I say no?" I asked. "What if I go to Carlos Jones and tell him everything you just said?"

She must have considered the possibility. She was obviously smart. She'd thought through everything before she came here. Every variable and every scenario. People like her, people like me, we had no choice. We had to be careful, to make sure we covered every base. If we didn't, we risked leaving ourselves exposed. The moment we did, someone would take advantage. That was as inevitable as the sun rising. More so.

"You won't," she said.

"You said yourself, Chelsea is his weakness," Atlas said slowly. "That gives her a lot of leverage. She might take your place." He didn't seem to hate the idea.

Nyla turned to him slowly. "There's a difference between being his weakness and being his equal," she said bluntly. "He doesn't consider me either of those things, but I have his ear. She never will. He'd hear what she has to say and use her anyway. He considers most women to be nothing more than objects. It took me a long time and a lot of work for him to... I don't know, forget I'm female. He moved on to others and let me quietly work to get where I am now."

She sounded so clinical about it, my stomach turned. "How young were you?" I asked softly.

She pressed her mouth into a tight line. I thought she might not respond. Finally she said, "Seventeen."

"I think I want to cut his nuts off," Dallas said softly.

"Go get in line," Atlas said.

"You're the one who worked with him," I pointed out coldly.

"Pretended to," Atlas said. He looked meaningfully at Nyla.

She looked back at him. "Convincingly."

"He couldn't have been that convincing; you said all of that in front of him," Jay said. Apparently he knew who he believed, and it wasn't her. Or at least, his faith in Atlas was firmly back in place.

"That might have been a test, to see if he ran off and told Jones," I said. I cocked my head at Atlas.

"I'm not telling him Jack shit," Atlas said. "I want him taken down, too. Before he touches my woman. And Jay."

"Our woman," Dallas corrected.

"Yeah, our woman," Jay said. "Or any of us." His gaze slid to Nyla, including her in that, even though we hadn't come to any sort of agreement. Evidently, he decided she could be trusted. Or maybe he also saw her as our way out. "What do we do?"

"The first thing you need to do is get dressed." She stood up and put the chair back to the side of the room. "In an hour or so, he'll come here. We'll all be taken to a private airstrip and we'll board a plane. At least, that's his idea. We need to do everything we can to avoid getting on that aircraft."

"Unless you have a stash of guns..." I looked at her questioningly.

"Not that I can give you," Nyla said. "You need to do something more." Without skipping a beat, she told us what she had in mind.

"Hell no." Dallas sat up so fast, the sheet fell away from him. He grabbed it and jerked it back over his cock before pulling his pants back up from around his hips. "You can't be serious."

"Unless you can think of a better way." She looked at him sideways. She hadn't even glanced down at his body. All of her attention was focused on our faces and her plan.

"There has to be one." Atlas sat on the edge of the bed, beside Jay. "There's too much that could go wrong this way. It's too big a risk." He chewed over that silently before asking, "What happens if we get on that plane?"

"We end up somewhere else I can't control." Nyla ran the tip of her finger up and down her thigh, just over her phone.

I shook my head. "He's not going to buy it. He knows I know he killed my boyfriends. He's not going to think I've turned to him that quickly."

"He will if you're a good enough actor," she said. "Which I know you are. You spent years pretending to be attracted to strange men while you danced for them. Pretending to enjoy it when they fucked you. You can pretend to be into him if you have to."

I grimaced. She was right, I did all of that. If I had to, I could make him think I enjoyed fucking him, but the idea made me sick.

"How do I know you'll intervene in time?" I asked.

Dallas grabbed my arm. "You can't be serious.

You can't do this. We'll get on that plane. We'll find some other time and place to deal with him. The next time I see him, I can strangle him." His troubled eyes pleaded with me to do anything but this.

"Then you'll be dead," Nyla said.

"I don't care," he snapped. "As long as he doesn't touch Chelsea."

I slipped my arm around him and pulled him to me. "Losing Storm, Frost and Ramsey was enough. I can't lose you too. Even if I have to..." I couldn't finish the words. "Promise me you won't do anything that will get you killed."

"Considering what we're planning—" Nyla started.

I glared at her until she closed her mouth with a click of her teeth.

I turned back to Dallas. "I meant, don't take any unnecessary risks, especially not for me. We will get through this. We will."

I drew in a long breath and exhaled slowly, trying to think of the possible scenarios and how many ways this could end up a huge shit storm. Too many.

"Can you get the guys out while I distract him?" Seeing them safe and away might be worth doing whatever I had to do with Jones. I'd been selfish in letting Dallas come here in the first place. I wouldn't do that again. I'd put him first, no matter the cost to me.

"Maybe," Nyla said vaguely. "It would be better if they stayed and helped with this coup."

"We're staying," Atlas said. "There's no way in hell am leaving here without Chelsea."

"Me either," Jay said.

Dallas didn't say anything; he didn't need to. I knew nothing would convince him to leave, unless he was forced. Even then, he'd resist.

"I guess we're doing this," I said with a sigh. What could go wrong?

Only everything.

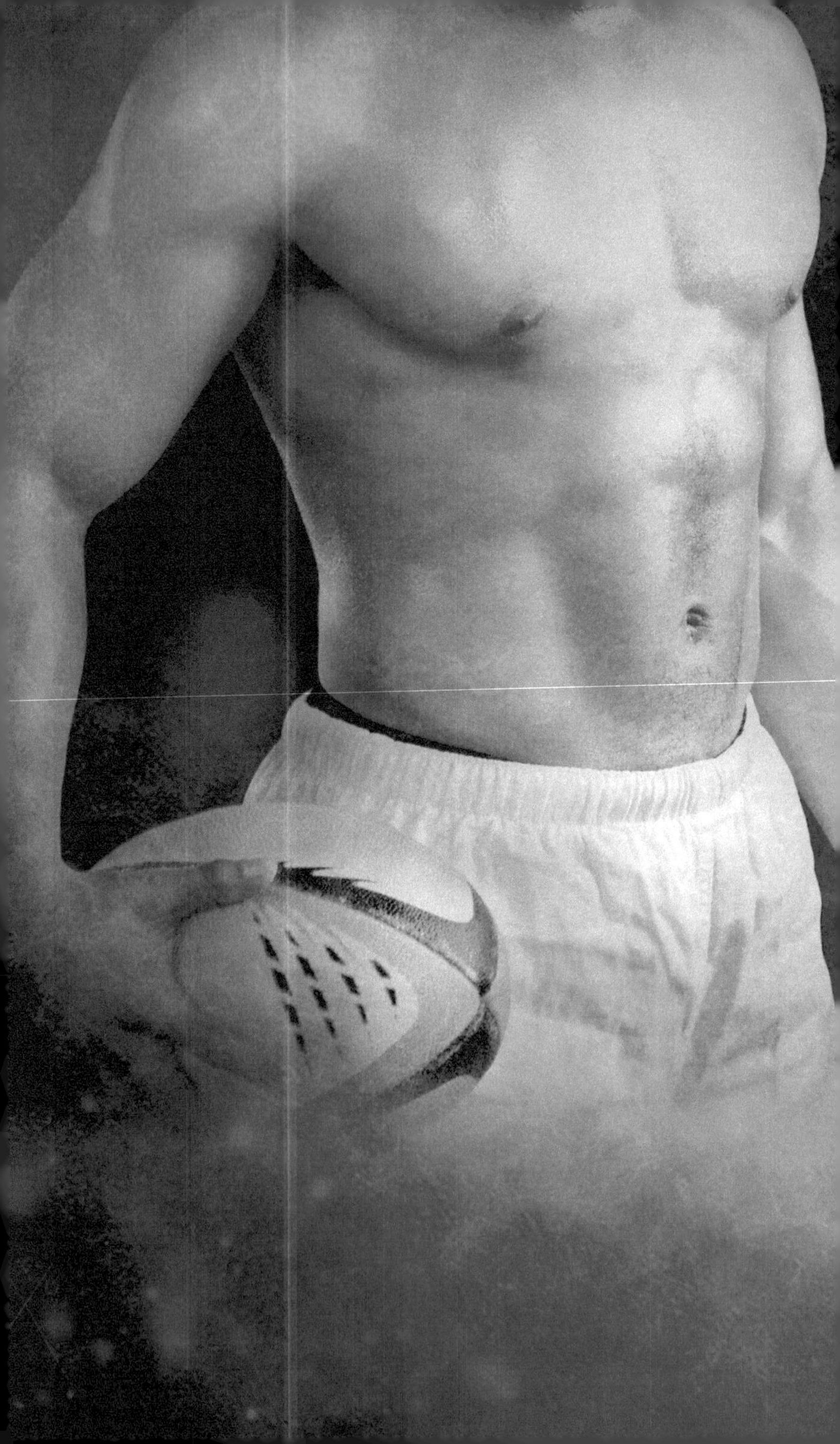

Chapter Thirteen

Chelsea

I managed a brief shower and change of clothes without being disturbed. The guys all took quick turns after me, barely getting under the water long enough to soap and rinse.

After about twenty minutes, we arrayed ourselves around the room. Dallas and I sitting side by side on the bed. Jay on a chair. Atlas reclined against the wall beside him, legs crossed at the ankles. He looked relaxed, but I knew he wasn't. He was as on guard as the rest of us. Waiting. Ready.

Finally, the click of the door came. Even though I was expecting it, I startled slightly.

Dallas squeezed my knee for reassurance.

I squeezed his in return. In spite of assurances from Nyla, I struggled to have faith in this plan of hers. Her visit could still have been nothing more than a ruse, to discourage me from fighting back.

Maybe I was being naïve, but I didn't think so. I genuinely believed her when she said she wanted to take down Carlos Jones. Those brief moments of vulnerability were peeks behind her mask. A façade she spent years building. One she had to keep in place to protect her life and her sanity. My heart hurt to think she'd spent this long biding her time, preparing for the right opportunity.

On the other hand, she had used me like I was some kind of toy. A puppet to be moved around however she wanted. I couldn't see them, but she still had her strings attached to me. Given half a chance, she'd tug on them again. Next time, I'd be ready. I'd push back. I wasn't going to let her, or anyone else, control me.

One of Jones' minions stepped into the room ahead of him. He glanced around to make sure it was safe before nodding to his boss.

Jones' gaze swept over all of us, taking us in one by one, before his gaze lingered on me. "I see you're ready to leave."

I rose slowly, forcing my mind to the headspace I used to be in when I was stripping. Provocative, sensual. Confident in my own skin. Storm's nickname for me was Panther. That's who I'd be. A cat, stalking her prey.

"I like it here," I said smoothly. "It's comfortable." I stepped toward him like I was back on that stage. I was the one in control here. He was the toy, he just didn't know it yet.

"I'm taking you somewhere better," he said. When I was close enough, he placed a finger under my chin. He didn't need to tilt it up to meet his gaze. Unlike my boyfriends, he was the same height as me. Tall, but not as tall as them.

"What's the hurry?" I tilted my head slightly, so as to avoid dislodging his finger. As much as I wanted to. Even this light touch felt slimy. Repugnant.

I reminded myself to switch off those thoughts and focus on what was really important. Getting out of here with everyone intact but Jones.

To be honest, not looking back at my guys was a struggle. I could almost feel them wanting to punch out Jones' lights. They mentally had their fingers wrapped around his throat, squeezing, squeezing.

"Dusk Bay is a cesspool," he said. "I'm sure you'd prefer to be somewhere other than here. I know I would."

"I like Dusk Bay." I pouted. "I thought for sure

you'd have one of those nice, big houses with a view of the bay."

He looked at me with undisguised suspicion. I could almost see the thoughts tumbling around in his brain. What was I up to, and did he care? If I was up to something, surely he'd be able to deal with it. Why not enjoy me while I was being agreeable?

Arrogant prick.

"I do have a house like that," he said. "But it's not the place for you right now. I want you away from here." The first hint of doubt flickered across his dark eyes. The longer I was here, the greater the chances my brother would find us. At least he was smart enough to be scared of Ice.

"That's so sweet," I purred. "Are you worried about me?" He was worried about his own ass, that was all. He only cared about what he could do to mine. I placed a hand on his chest and smiled.

He grabbed my wrist and held it firmly. "I don't waste time worrying. But I won't let anyone take what's mine."

Behind me, one of the guys let out a soft growl. I couldn't tell if it was Dallas or Jay. I knew it wasn't Atlas. Not when he was still pretending to be a dutiful minion. He was the only one who hadn't taken a shower. Instead, watching over us to make sure we continued to behave.

Jones chuckled. "I see we have some objection, but they'll learn. I own you now. In fact, now might be a good time for a demonstration. We have a few minutes before we have to leave for the airport." He slid his hand from my chin, my cheek and grabbed a fistful of hair. "Get on your knees."

I'd been issued that instruction so many times in the past, complying was almost automatic. I didn't need to think, just sank down, taking his hand with me, still tangled in my hair.

"Good girl," he said smoothly. "Take out my cock."

Judging by the size of the tent in his pants, I'd have to find it first.

I smiled up at him and reached for the tongue of his zipper.

The door burst open behind him.

"Sorry boss, but I thought you'd want to know. You were right about Nyla working against you."

Jones shoved me away from him as Nyla herself was pushed through the door in front of a couple of his men. I scooted back to the bed, beside Dallas.

Nyla staggered, but just managed to keep her

feet. "I didn't do anything. You can't prove a thing." Her eyes were firmly on Jones.

One of his minions held out a phone and tapped on the screen. Her voice filled the room.

"Because he had my parents killed. They stood in his way. He wanted me and my sisters to belong to the cartel. In every sense of the word. So I pretended to be a dutiful woman. I managed to get his trust and work my way up, through the ranks. Stepping on anyone and everyone that had a part in my parents' murder, as I went. Carlos Jones is the last of them. But he's also the most difficult. He's always surrounded by other people. Oh, I could shoot him in the head, but then I'd be killed too. No, I need to separate him from them, and find a way they can't retaliate until I take over."

Nyla's face paled. Her eyes narrowed and she glanced at us.

"We didn't record that," I said. "He took our phones before we were brought here."

"I suspected you were up to something and put an extra microphone in here," Jones said. "One you didn't know about."

"She turned the rest of them off," the minion said helpfully. "So she could go behind your back."

"I was trying to gain their trust," Nyla hedged. "Make things easier for you."

I wasn't even slightly surprised she'd turn on us so quickly. Of course she was looking after her own ass.

"It worked, didn't it?" she continued. "She was on her knees, ready to suck you off." She gave me a look like I was repulsive in some way. As if it was my idea.

Jones stared at her for at least a minute, before raising his hand and slapping her across the face. He hit her so hard, she staggered back into the man behind her. He grabbed her arm to keep her from falling.

"Ungrateful bitch," he snarled. "I should have killed you too. You were always more trouble than you were worth."

She stood looking defiant, her hand over her cheek. "I should have killed you when I had the chance. Even if I was dead right after, it would've been worth it. The world would be rid of you."

His face turned red. "I should have you taken out and shot like the dog you are. But I'm not going to. Instead, you're coming with me. It seems I haven't taught you well enough. You've forgotten who owns you." To his minions he added, "If she opens her mouth again, shut her up with your cock."

"Will do, boss," one of the henchmen said. He seemed to be looking forward to it, hoping she'd give him an excuse.

Nyla recoiled in revulsion, but pressed her lips tightly together.

For the first time, I saw real fear on her face. It wasn't an empty threat. Jones would let his men rape her if she said another word.

Taking my cue from her, I made sure my mouth was closed, and nestled as close to Dallas as I dared. I knew it might piss Jones off, but right now I needed the physical comfort his presence provided.

Jones glanced at us, but if he noticed or cared, he didn't say anything. "Get them all in the cars. It's past time we left for the airport. Atlas, I hold you personally responsible for the actions of the other three." He flicked his fingers roughly in our direction.

"If any of you put your foot out of line, he can look forward to a bullet in his brain." His gaze lingering on me. He wasn't going to put up with trouble from any of us. Nyla well and truly pissed him off. Now, he was on his guard.

"Understood, boss," Atlas said smoothly. "They'll behave."

"They better." Jones shouldered past Nyla and stalked out of the room without glancing back.

"Grab your stuff and let's go," Atlas told us. "We don't want to annoy him any further."

I very much wanted to annoy him, but now seemed like a bad time to do it. I had no doubt he'd kill Atlas and not think twice about it.

Instead, I stood and grabbed my bag before filing out of the room between Dallas and Jay.

At some point in the not so distant future, I was going to have words with Nyla Fox.

Thanks to her, we were deeper in the shit than we were before.

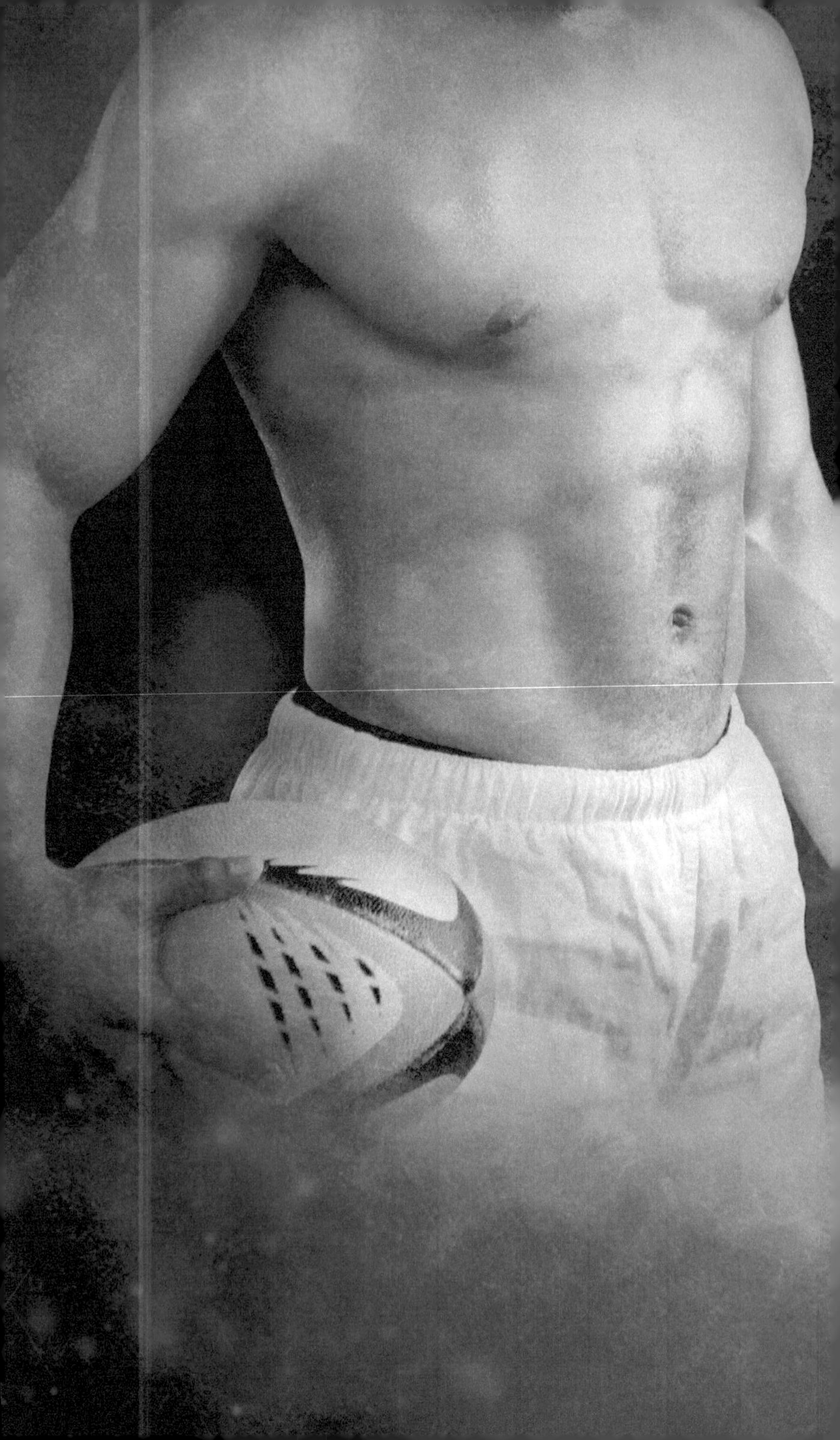

Chapter Fourteen

Chelsea

We were bundled into the back seat of a different SUV from the one which brought us here the night before. This was the kind with seating for seven. Two of Jones' henchmen sat in the rear two seats, behind Dallas, Jay and I, who sat in the middle. Atlas sat beside the driver.

I briefly glimpsed Nyla being pushed into a car in front of us, and Jones himself getting into a third.

In a convoy of an eventual five cars, we drove away from the small house, and back on the highway.

I couldn't help glancing roughly in the direction of Frost's property. Had anyone gone there yet? Had they found their bodies? Did they realise we weren't there, or did they assume we were dead too, incinerated into ash?

To be realistic, if anyone went there already, the debris would be too hot to uncover anything. That would have to wait for at least a day or two. They'd have to wait and search for our remains when the place cooled. Only then would they know we were gone.

If anyone went there at all. Chances were, they hadn't. No one would have started to miss us yet. If Sadie was still in Dusk Bay, she might have. But she wasn't, and everyone else was busy with their lives. Sooner or later, they'd figure it out, but by then it might be too late.

"I'm glad you didn't do that," Dallas whispered, breaking through my thoughts. "Suck his cock," he added a moment later. "I don't think I would have been able to stop myself from ripping him to pieces."

"Me too," Jay whispered. "That was— You would have done it if you had to, wouldn't you?"

"I'd do anything to get us out of there alive," I said. Even choking on his cock. Even letting him slam himself into my pussy. I'd hate every second of it, but I'd force a smile and think of my guys. They were my priority, nothing else.

"Fuck, Chels." Dallas' fingers tightened around my thigh. "This is bullshit."

"You really think she was working with us at all?"

Jay asked. "Nyla, I mean." He seemed particularly uncomfortable, crowded against the door. Trying to give himself some space. A couple of times I thought he might lose his shit, but he'd clung onto it for now. He was tough as hell and I loved him for it.

I shook my head. "I don't know. I think so, but she has an angle of her own." Who the hell didn't? "I think she wants him gone, but she'll throw us under the bus to take care of herself."

"Yeah, I figured," Jay said. "She backpedalled pretty fast when he found out."

"Yeah, she did," I agreed. I was almost grateful they'd discovered what she did. If they hadn't, I'd have the taste of his cum in my mouth right now. Or the feel of it wet between my thighs.

I shuddered.

"I don't trust her," Dallas said. "She'll get us killed if we're not careful."

"Then we be careful," Jay said. "I don't trust her either. I believe her when she said what happened to her, but like Chels said, she's looking after herself."

"She's definitely doing that." I sighed. Why wouldn't she? She had no reason to trust us either. We could just as easily turn on her if it suited us.

Honestly, if it did, I wasn't sure I'd hesitate. If—*when*—we got out of here, it might be by screwing her over. I hoped that wouldn't be the case, but if it was, that was what we'd do.

"Could we wait until the car slows down, and..." Dallas jerked his head towards the door beside him.

"Don't fucking try it," one of the minions growled from behind him. "The boss doesn't need you with knees."

His companion laughed as though that was actually funny. "He needs her with knees, so she can kneel in front of him."

"Bitch can kneel in front of me anytime," the first minion said.

"Which one?" the second asked. "This one, or Nyla?"

"Who cares?" the first responded. "A mouth is a mouth. I'd come down both of their throats."

I made a mental note that, if I got a chance, I would kill both of them first.

That thought was followed by the unfriendly reminder I'd never killed anyone. That might change, and it might change soon. If it had to happen, I couldn't hesitate. If I did, I'd be the dead one instead. Or my remaining guys would.

"I'm going to rip their fucking arms off," Dallas said in a harsh whisper.

"So am I," Jay said.

"Shhh," I urged. "Don't give them an excuse to do anything to you."

"You better listen to her," the first minion said. "Because we would take the excuse if it arose. Jones wouldn't give a shit if we killed you right now. The only thing he's interested in is her pussy."

"And her mouth," the second added. "I've lost track of the amount of woman I've seen blow him off. It was even consensual a time or two." He laughed.

"Yeah, his favourite thing is a woman on her knees." The first minion chuckled. "Come to think of it, it's mine too. Far as I'm concerned, that's where women belong."

How enlightened of them.

I rolled my eyes, knowing they couldn't see. The Crimson Vipers weren't known for being high up on the evolutionary scale. The best thing that could happen to them would be to have a woman in charge. She'd change a lot of things, starting with bullshit like this.

"I get the impression we hurt her feelings," one of them sneered. He leaned forward until he was breathing down my neck. "You might as well toughen up now, sweetheart. None of us gives a shit about your feelings. You're nothing but a body for Jones to fuck, and us when he's done with you. Don't worry, that won't take long. He usually gets bored within a week or two. At that point, I'll introduce you to my cock. I'm going to fuck your mouth until you gag, and then fuck it some more. If you're lucky, I might even do it while Eddie here fucks that pussy of yours. Don't think any of this is a threat. It's a when, not an if. We always get Jones' leftovers when he's done with them. Eddie, how many times have you fucked Nyla?"

"I dunno. A shit ton," Eddie said. "I like it better when she fights back though. Like that last one."

The longer they spoke, the more my stomach turned. I wished I thought they were full of it, but I believed every word they said.

The Crimson Vipers had no respect for women. They bought and sold them for a reason. Hearing it like this was something else. I wanted to destroy every last one of them. Starting with Jones.

No, I corrected myself. I wanted to leave him until last. He could watch me burn down everything around him before I killed him too.

I placed a hand on one of Dallas' arms and one of Jay's too, to keep them from leaping over the back of the seat and throttling both men.

Neither would get any further than removing their seat belts before the minions pulled out guns and used them. Right now, it was nothing more than words. We could ignore words.

When it became more than that... I doubted I'd be able to hold them back, even if I wanted to.

Nyla might not get us killed. We might do it ourselves.

By the time we reached the airfield, an hour later, my body was getting sore from sitting still and stiff.

The guys quietly seethed the entire time, barely keeping themselves contained. Not only were they angry, they also weren't used to sitting still for too long. Outside flights, they didn't have to do it often. Usually, they were active all day, training and playing. Right now, they were bundles of jangled nerves, coiled like a spring waiting to be released. Tired of being stuck inside a box.

"We can do this," I whispered. "We need to play it cool. That's the only way we get through this, okay?"

"I can try," Dallas murmured.

Jay nodded once, unconvincingly.

I squeezed their arms and looked out the window. Searching for an escape route, or a weapon. Something.

The airstrip itself was tiny and insignificant, just a single runway and a couple of big hangars.

A small jet sat near a hangar, its engine off for now. This was the kind of aircraft that would carry twenty or thirty people at most. Of course, anything bigger than that wouldn't be able to land here. The trees were too close for a big airliner to manoeuvre, much less take off and land. Even in something small, it would be tricky.

A few cars were parked beside a distant hangar. Presumably belonging to the maintenance staff who worked at the airport.

Jones' men climbed out of the lead vehicles and hurried about, readying the plane.

My heart sank, but I couldn't let despair get to me. That would be the easiest way for Jones to win. He wasn't going to win and he wasn't going to break any of us. He could try, and I knew he would, but he'd fail. So would the assholes who were now herding us out of the SUV and across the tarmac.

I looked back in the direction of the highway, hoping like hell to see a bigger convoy of cars than the one we arrived in.

None came.

Without a word, we were pushed towards the

steps leading up to the plane and inside, Nyla right in front of me.

She managed a brief, regretful look before letting herself be shoved with the rest of us.

Eddie slapped her ass, but she only dropped her head and kept on walking. If her body language was an indication, she wanted to turn and punch him off the steps, but she didn't dare. She knew what would happen if she did.

If I could, I'd try to make sure she got out of here with us. She'd make a better leader for the Crimson Vipers than anyone else I'd seen so far. If there was anything left to lead once I was finished with them.

I'd make no guarantees there would be. If there wasn't, I'd find her a place somewhere in this world. No doubt she'd tell me she was perfectly capable of looking after herself, but if she needed me to, I'd try. That was all I could promise right now.

To try.

"Boss!" one of the minions called out. "We've got company."

Chapter Fifteen

Ramsey

THE BUILDING WAS A NONDESCRIPT SHED, A couple of kilometres outside the limits of Dusk Bay. Several cars were already parked outside the front when we pulled up.

"Are you sure this is the place?" Storm peered through the front windscreen. His brow was creased, grey eyes swiping back and forth doubtfully.

"This is the address he sent me." If only to prove I had faith in Ice, I pushed out of the car and started toward the structure.

For half a second, I entertained the same doubt, but there was no reason for Chelsea's brother to send us to the wrong place. If he had, it was only to keep us out of the way, so we didn't get harmed. Instinct told me that wasn't what was going on here.

That was confirmed when I stepped through the open double doors. The heavy smell of fuel and grease lingered in the air, along with a heavier dose of barely contained anger. That radiated from Chelsea's brother, Ice, and to a lesser extent the men standing with him.

Ice glanced over to me and gave me the slightest hint of a nod to acknowledge my presence. He was smiling, like usual, but no one would miss the fury in his eyes. He was ready to hurt people.

He looked away and resumed his conversation. "Thanks for coming. You guys look like shit." He elbowed one of the Brantley twins, who elbowed him back.

"Bro, you try having three-month-old twins and see how you go. It's exhausting, right, Park?"

"I can't remember the last time I had a full night's sleep," Hunter replied wearily. "But the little guys are worth it. Hey, Ramsey, good to see you. Shame the circumstances are crap." He walked over to give me a side hug.

"Who are your friends?" Parker asked. He looked around us to the doorway. "Hey, I know you guys! Storm Keller and Daniel Frost. I'm a big fan of the Smashers. I've been trying to convince Mack to sell us the team for ages now, right Hunter?"

Hunter squinted at him. "Since when?"

Parker grinned. "I don't know, but I'm going to nag him now."

"We already own the Dusk Bay Demons," Hunter reminded him. "Why do we need another team?"

"The question is why *wouldn't* we need another team?" Parker shrugged. "Who else is coming to this party?"

"Who the hell are these guys?" Storm asked.

Hunter and Parker exchanged looks of mock outrage. At least, I thought it was mock.

"You haven't heard of us?" Parker asked. "Apparently we need to invest in more publicity. Maybe a billboard. We could have them all over Dusk Bay, and on the highway coming in from north and south. Maybe coming from the west as well."

"We're not getting billboards, Park," Hunter said. He offered his hand to Storm. "Hunter Brantley. My brother Parker." He jerked his head towards his twin.

"Brantley?" Storm frowned. "Like that Reuben Brantley guy?"

The twins exchanged another look before cracking up laughing.

"Dibs on telling Reuben he referred to him like that," Parker said, mid-laugh.

"Dibs on being there to watch," Hunter added.

Storm shook his head like they were both out of their minds. He leaned over to me and said, "Are these guys supposed to help us get Chelsea back?"

"Don't be fooled," Ice said. "They act like a pair of clowns, but they're both almost as ruthless as I am. They're Reuben Brantley's youngest brothers."

"And favourite brothers," Hunter said. "Also most indispensable, if I may say so myself."

"I don't know, Caleb is pretty indispensable," Parker said. After a beat, they both laughed again.

"Pair of clowns is right," Storm said darkly.

"They seem like fun to me," Frost remarked.

"We are fun." Parker draped an arm over Frost's shoulder. "We also understand the gravity of the situation. We will get Chelsea back. We like her. She reminds me a lot of Lila, our girlfriend. Smart, determined and kick-ass."

"She's all of those things," Ice said.

"I bet she's looking for a way to escape before we even get there," Hunter said. "Lila did that the time she was taken by some asshole. We got there to rescue her, but she'd already rescued herself." He smiled softly. Clearly he adored her.

"Chelsea's definitely a badass," I said. If anyone could save themselves, it was her, but without knowing where Atlas and Jay stood, I could only assume the odds were not currently in her favour. We'd change that.

"She's the biggest badass," Ice said. "The only one who doesn't think so is her." He glanced over to the doorway as another couple of cars pulled up and footsteps headed closer.

"Who are we killing?" Gianni asked cheerfully as he stepped into the shed. He was followed by Mina DiMarco and Daisy LaSalle, along with a bunch of other men.

"What he said." Daze jerked a thumb towards Gianni. "Who the hell dared take my friend?"

"Carlos Jones," Ice said simply.

"Ah," Gianni replied. "Well, he should have died a long time ago." He gave Mina a sideways glance and a smile.

She didn't disagree with him. "What's the plan?" she said instead.

"Do we know where he took her?" Daze asked. She looked ready to slice open throats and ask questions later.

"I've been communicating with some contacts," Ice said. "Calling in every favour I have. A friend of a friend of a friend said she was in a property close to Dusk Bay last night. That same friend of a friend of a friend said he was planning to fly her out this morning."

"I suspect you're not suggesting we have a dogfight with his aircraft." Parker looked disappointed.

"Not while Chelsea's on it," I said before anyone started to think that was viable idea.

"Abso-fucking-lutely not," Storm said. "I don't give a shit what you do to Jones and how you kill him, but if you get Chelsea killed, I'm going to come after every last one of you."

"I like him," Parker loudly whispered to Hunter. "He's got balls. I don't mean footballs either."

"I didn't think you did, Park," Hunter whisper-shouted back. "I like him too. I think we should try to buy the Smashers."

"I'm not saying that's not important, but can we focus on the matter at hand?" Daze gave them both a meaningful look. "Why are we here, Ice? Why aren't we at the airport?"

"That's a very good question," Storm said. "Why the fuck are we wasting time here?" He looked ready to run straight back to the SUV and floor it.

Ice raised his hands and gestured around him. "We are at the airport. It might not look like it, but this is one of the hangars they use to repair aircraft."

The hangar was full of tools, which hung on the walls and lay neatly on workbenches. Now I knew what to look for, I saw smears of oil on the concrete floor, here and there. It also explained the smell that hit me the moment I stepped inside.

"I think it looks like it," Parker said.

"Me too," Hunter agreed. "I'm guessing you have a plan." He rubbed his hands together in anticipation.

"How do we know she hasn't left yet?" Storm demanded.

"Because I've been here for hours, and no planes have arrived or left." If Ice was irritated by his question, he gave no sign. Instead, he was all business. "According to my contact, we have approximately an hour. We have to wait here until the aircraft arrives. If they see us, they'll circle around and leave. Once they do that, we might not get another chance."

"There are cars outside," Daze pointed out.

"That's a risk we have to take." Ice didn't look happy about it. "When the time comes, we have to be ready to jump back into our vehicles and drive. If we move the cars further away, we risk not being close enough. I'm not going to watch the plane take off again with my sister in it."

Gianni put a hand on his shoulder. "We won't let

that happen. Maybe we can park a couple of cars inside here, just to cut down the number of them. It'll only take a second or two more to drive back out."

"That's a good idea," Mina told him, her fondness for him showing in her blue eyes.

I'd rarely seen her show any kind of emotion. Seeing it now spoke volumes. She was easily one of the most contained, mysterious people I'd ever met. Anyone with any sense didn't turn their back on her. I didn't know why, exactly, but I knew she was dangerous.

"I have those from time to time." Gianni grinned. "I'll bring mine in here."

"So will I." Daze followed him out, keys jangling from her fingers.

"That's it?" Storm asked. "We just have to wait?"

"We can wait," Frost said. "This is Chelsea we're talking about. I'll wait for as long as it takes."

"I will too," I said. I didn't like it either, but if it wasn't for Ice, we wouldn't even have this lead. I wouldn't let myself think what would happen if this somehow slipped through our fingers. Jones could take her anywhere in the world and we may never find her again.

If that was the case, I'd never give up looking. I

knew the others wouldn't either. Fuck football. We'd spend the rest of our lives searching if we had to.

"I mean, I'm not going anywhere," Storm conceded. Except to step out of the way when Gianni drove through the wide doorway and parked to one side of the hangar. Daze followed a few moments later. That left three cars parked outside. Suspicious, but less suspicious than five.

Once they turned off the engines, we were plunged into silence, apart from the sound of birds and the occasional scuff of feet on the floor.

My heart beat steadily through my body. I focused on that. Keep calm. Wait patiently. Be ready.

I wasn't sure who heard it first, but we all drew ourselves up a little straighter, faces turned towards the doorway. Bodies stiff and still.

I wasn't sure if I was hearing things, but then the sound became louder.

A plane engine.

"This is it," Ice whispered. "Wait for my go."

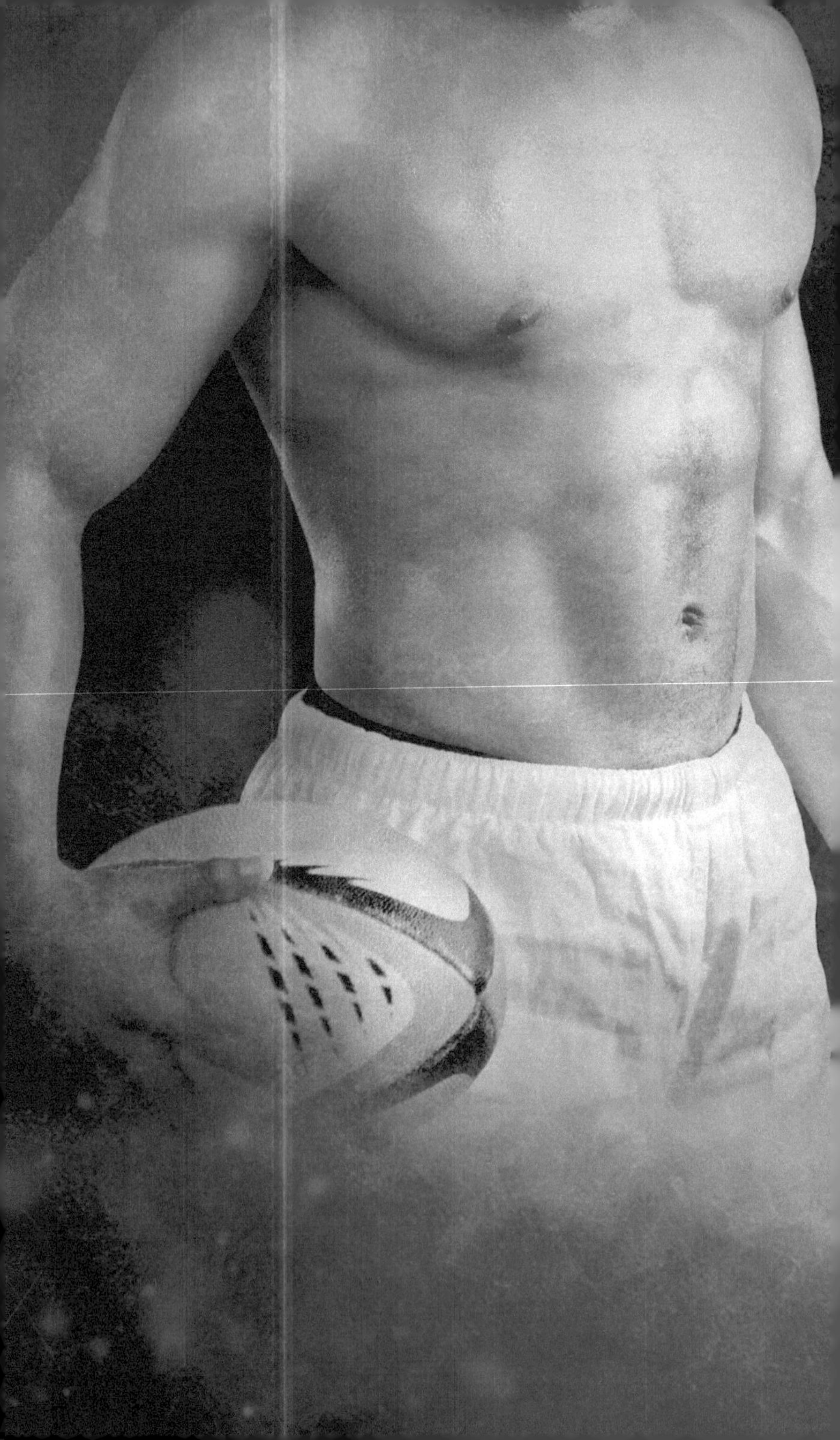

Chapter Sixteen

Chelsea

I held on to Dallas' arm, my gaze out the window at the approaching vehicles. Five of them, all dark. Three sedans and two SUVs. If I didn't know better, I'd think one of those SUVs was...

I couldn't let myself think it. If I did, I'd get my hopes up. I couldn't let that happen, in case they were dashed again. I couldn't, yet...

The vehicles were moving fast, headed directly towards us. There was no doubt in my mind they were here for us.

No doubt in anyone else's either, by the way Jones shouted.

"Get this bird off the ground!" He glared at the flight crew, who didn't jump fast enough to do as he said. He pulled a gun from his hip and aimed it at the closest of them. "Now."

"Yes, sir," the man squeaked, and hurried toward the door.

In the corner of my eye, I saw Nyla, her lips moving as she counted down slowly. When she reached three, she looked at me and nodded.

"Two. One."

The car skidded to a halt beside the plane, kicking up another storm of dust before they reached the tarmac.

I squeezed Dallas' hand and threw off my seatbelt; he did the same.

I was vaguely aware of Nyla rising and sprinting to the front of the aircraft, slipping between the curtain that separated the front from the back.

Together, Dallas and I charged the closest minion, grabbing him, one on either side. Hands on his shoulders, we slammed his head into the window behind him.

He let out a cry of pain and blinked, dazed from the blow. That was enough for us to grab his gun, which I took from Dallas' hesitant fingers.

Without thinking, I pressed the barrel of the gun against the man's forehead and pulled the trigger.

Time stopped.

They say you never forget your first kill. As long as I lived, I'd never forget the bang of the gun. The way it recoiled in my hand. I swear I felt the bullet leave the barrel and slam into bone and brain.

I saw the exact moment of impact. The exact moment he died. His eyes wide, he slumped down to the floor of the aircraft.

Time resumed.

Atlas punched another minion in the face before grabbing his weapon and shooting him in the heart.

Jay was wrestling with a third, the gun between them. Their hands swung wildly from one direction to the other, at times pointing at us, and others pointing away.

In the middle of this, Dallas ducked under their arms and threw himself, tackling the minion to the floor. They both landed with a grunt and Jay was forced to let go of the gun.

The minion pointed the weapon at Dallas' face and ground out, "Get the fuck off me."

Hands raised to either side, Dallas rolled and climbed to his feet. He stepped back while the henchmen rose.

"Put down your weapons," he minion ordered. He aimed the gun at me.

I quickly weighed up my options and knew Atlas

was doing the same. Could we shoot him before he shot one of us?

"I said, put down your weapons," the henchmen growled.

"Jones won't be happy if you shoot his trophy," Atlas pointed out.

"I'll shoot you then." The henchmen turned his gun toward Atlas. "Put your weapons down."

Past him, I saw people climbing out of the cars. I immediately recognised my brother and the Brantley twins. How the hell did they know we were here? And Daisy LaSalle. Mina DiMarco and Gianni as well.

And...

I turned my head and stared. I must be dead, because I was seeing something impossible.

Storm, Frost and Ramsey were all headed to the side of the plane, guns in hand.

Alive.

I'd never seen anything more beautiful, or hotter, in my life.

"Looks like you didn't blow them up after all," Atlas said, nodding towards the window.

The tiny moment of distraction when the minion also turned to look was all I needed.

In a snap, I had the gun raised, aimed and fired.

The bullet hit him square in the chest, throwing him back against the seat beside him.

We all ducked down between the seats, in legroom that would have been incredible on a commercial flight.

"Nyla?" I called out. For a relatively small aircraft, I wasn't sure what was happening in the front of it.

"Little help here. If you're not busy," she called back.

"Fucking bitch," Jones snarled. That was followed by a gunshot that made me wince. Did that come from her, or was it aimed at her?

"Stay here," Atlas told us.

"Not a chance," I replied. "I'm going with you." I wasn't going to stay here in the back and wait for them to come to us.

He rolled his eyes towards the ceiling, but eventually sighed out his nose and stood. "Fine, stay behind me."

I didn't want to do that either, but he was big enough to take up most of the aisle, unless I tried to elbow him aside. Which would do nothing but waste time.

Gun held firmly in my hand, I followed him toward the front of the plane.

Atlas pulled aside the curtain with the tip of his finger, peering through the gap he made. After a moment, he shoved it aside, out of the way.

Nyla and Carlos Jones stood behind seats on either side of the aisle. Each had a gun in their hand, both aimed at each other.

Beyond them, several men did the same, clearly having taken one side or the other.

"You're not getting out of here alive," Jones said. Without taking his eyes off her, he ordered, "Get this aircraft in the air."

"You're outnumbered," I pointed out. "Give me one good reason why we shouldn't kill you."

"I'll kill her first," he said.

"Why should I care?" I asked. "I want to get off this plane, and I want you dead. What difference does it make to me if she lives or dies?"

"Because you're a doctor," he said. "Are you going to let a woman die so you can go free?"

I hated to admit it, he had a point. I didn't want Nyla to die. She told me she had something up her sleeve and to trust her. I knew without doubt she was the one who told my brother where to find us. I didn't know how, but she had. She waited until they arrived and used that as a distraction to fight back. She told me to wait for her signal and I had. The only thing that hadn't gone the way she planned was that Jones was still alive.

In everything else, she was the puppet master again. This time, I didn't mind.

"I can tell by your silence that I'm right," he boasted. "Put down your weapons and back away. No one else needs to die today."

The plane's engine started to hum.

Jones smiled. "It seems like we're leaving after all. How nice of the Brantley family to send people to wave us goodbye."

"It's really nice of them to send Storm, Frost and Ramsey," I said. "Especially when you said you killed them."

A flash of surprise crossed his face, but he didn't waver. "I'll do better next time."

The aircraft started to roll across the tarmac.

"There won't be a next time," I said.

"If you so much as aim a gun at me, I'll kill her," Jones warned.

"I forgive you if you have to," Nyla said. "Don't let him take you."

I glanced at Atlas, giving him a silent message to be ready. He'd have to be quick if we were going to pull this off. If he wasn't, Nyla would be dead.

"I guess I'll do this then." I pointed the gun straight up and squeezed the trigger.

Chapter Seventeen

Chelsea

THE MOMENTARY DISTRACTION OF ME SHOOTING a bullet into the ceiling of the aircraft was all they needed.

Atlas shot the gun out of Jones' hand with precision a surgeon would be proud of.

At the same time, Nyla shot Jones in the foot.

He cried out loud in pain and surprise, shaking his hand and pulling his foot back towards himself.

"Fucking hell!" He threw himself down as his minions, and those working with Nyla, used the same distraction to fire at each other. A couple of shots and all that were left were Nyla's men, and mine.

The aircraft rolled to a stop, but the engine was still running.

I looked at Atlas questioningly, but he shrugged and stepped over a couple of bodies to tap on the cockpit door.

Nyla put away her gun and grabbed a set of handcuffs one of her men pulled out of his pocket and handed to her. She dangled them from her outstretched finger, right in front of Jones' face.

"There's two ways this goes down. You come willingly, or we hold you down and put these on you."

"Fuck off," he snarled. He eyed his gun, which still lay on the floor a few metres from him.

Before he could make a move, I dropped down to scoop it up. "There's a third option," I said.

"You let me walk away from here and I'll leave you alone," he said. He held the side of his shoe, his thumb pressed down on where the bullet must still be lodged. He was trying to stop from showing how much pain he was in. Trying, but failing.

The doctor in me wanted to help him, to take the bullet out. The rest of me wanted to put another bullet in him, not in his foot.

"I think we all know that wasn't the third option I had in mind," I said.

"I know it wasn't," Dallas said, coming up behind me.

"I do too." Jay trailed Dallas.

"You don't have the guts," Jones sneered. "You'd rather fix my foot. You know why? Because you're weak. Women don't have what it takes to get the job done. That's why I know you won't kill me. Neither will Nyla. You're both too soft."

"That's bullshit," I said flatly. "Believe me when I say it takes more strength to resist the very great temptation to kill you than it would to pull the trigger again. This way, you get to pay for the things you've done. For what you wanted to do to me. What you did to Nyla. To fuck knows how many other women."

"You can try," he said derisively. "We both know the Crimson Vipers will come and get me."

"They have to know where you are first," Nyla said. "And that place has to be somewhere they'd dare to go. Somewhere they didn't risk being chained up beside you." She glanced at me to indicate she was referring to my brother's workroom. If anyone was in any doubt.

"Isaac would have fun with him," I said.

"Speaking of Ice, you should come and see this," Atlas said from the cockpit.

With Nyla and four of her men standing over

Jones, guns aimed at his head, I figured it was safe to leave them to it for a few moments.

I stepped around them and moved to join Atlas. "What is it?" I peered out of the front windscreen of the aircraft.

My brother stood on the runway, Hunter and Parker beside him. Storm, Frost and Ramsey stood on the other side. They all had guns trained on the pilot.

"I figured we should stop," the pilot said nervously.

"Good call," Atlas said. He waved back as Ice waved at him, then at me when he saw me standing at Atlas' shoulder.

He looked relieved to see me alive and in one piece. Admittedly, I was a little teary now. They would all have risked themselves to stop the plane from taking off. They could have been mowed down.

When the twins and my boyfriends realised I was there, they all started waving frantically and smiling.

"Only these guys," I said softly, and waved back with slightly less energy. Right now, I wanted a long soak in the bath and a bottle of wine. Not to mention hugs from all of my ruck boys.

"We all love you," Atlas said. He put an arm around me and kissed my temple.

"I love all of you too," I said.

To the pilot I added, "I wouldn't try flying this until you have the bullet hole looked at. Just in case it breached the hull. Or whatever the outside of the aircraft is called."

Flying an unpressurised plane above a certain altitude could be deadly. Which was exactly why I fired into the ceiling. No matter how desperate Jones got, he wasn't going to risk flying in a damaged plane. He never would have risked himself.

The pilot sighed and turned off the engine, letting it putter before it finally fell silent.

"I'm just hired to fly this aircraft. I don't know anything about the person that chartered it." He held his hands to either side.

"Then you won't mind us checking," Atlas said.

"Go ahead," the pilot said. If he was innocent as he said he was, he could walk away. With a cover story, of course.

"I said fuck off," Jones snarled from behind us.

I turned to see three of Nyla's men trying to wrangle him down onto his stomach and pull his arms behind his back. He was wriggling and shoving, trying to fight them off.

"He might be right," I said so only Atlas could hear. "The cartel could try to rescue him."

To the side, Dallas and Jay were opening the aircraft door and trying to work out how to lower the steps to the ground.

"They won't succeed," Atlas said, looking in the same direction I was. "The cartel, I mean. Jay and Dallas are all over getting the steps down."

"Yes, they are," I said. Although, it looked as though they were about to Google how to do it. "Can you be so sure about the cartel? If people want something desperately enough, they'll do anything. He's their leader."

"Not anymore he's not." Atlas gaze slid to Nyla, who hadn't moved in the last handful of minutes. The barrel of her gun was still aimed firmly at Jones' head.

"You really think they'll accept that while he's still alive?" I asked. Not that men were ever misogynistic or anything.

"You really think he'll be alive that long?" Atlas countered.

"A day or two might be all it takes," I said.

Dallas and Jay finally had the steps down and Storm, Frost and Ramsey hurried up to greet them.

"Asshole!" Storm pointed his gun at Atlas. "Give me one good reason I shouldn't kill you right now."

"He's on our side," I said. "He was pretending to be with them."

Storm's brows dipped. "Are you sure? He could be pretending right now."

"I'm certain," I assured him. "I promise."

Storm lowered the gun a fraction. "What about that asshole?" He pointed the barrel toward Jones.

"Definitely not on our side," I said. "He's a horrible excuse for a human being and deserves to suffer."

Jones took the distraction we offered. He kicked one of the men trying to hold him down, in the groin, and threw off the other one. Leaping to his feet, he lunged at Nyla.

He managed to push her back against the side of the aircraft opposite the door, where the tiny galley kitchen was. The impact knocked the gun from her hand. He wrapped his hands around her throat and squeezed.

She wriggled, trying to get free. Her face turned pink, eyes wide with fear and frustration. She'd come so close, only to die now?

Not on my watch.

Feeling a bit like Lara Croft, I raised both of the

guns in my hands, aimed and shot Jones in the back of the head. The force of both bullets slammed through his skull, into his brain, killing him and sending blood and shards of bone flying.

He released his grip on Nyla and sagged slowly before slumping to the floor.

"There goes my Tuesday night entertainment," Ice remarked as he stepped into the aircraft.

"Sorry, not sorry," I said, exhaling on the last word.

Both of the guns slipped from my hands and I started to tremble. I found myself caught up in a tangle of arms and muscle as I started to fall.

Chapter Eighteen

Ramsey

I held back beside Dallas while the others all hugged and kissed Chelsea. Someone had to stay close enough to him to make sure he didn't fuck her right there in front of everyone. He would have, and we all knew it. Even while the plane stank of death.

Even on a cool day like today, the smell was going to get worse as the day wore on.

Without waiting to be asked, I called for a cleanup crew to take care of the bodies before anyone came along and started asking questions. This was a private airfield, but stranger things had happened. We didn't want to have to kill innocent members of the public because they saw too much.

Finally, Storm and Frost stepped back, giving me a chance to shoulder my way through to her. I wrapped my arms around her and pulled her so we were pressed hard against each other. I nestled my face into her neck, feeling her pulse beat against my cheek. I sent off a thought of gratitude to whatever higher power existed that she was still alive and seemingly unhurt.

"I didn't get a chance to ask how you guys survived the cottage exploding," she said softly. Trust her to be more worried about us than herself. She was always so giving and sweet.

"We weren't inside," I told her. "We were about to leave. A couple of minutes earlier and we wouldn't be here."

I ran my hand down her hair, tangling my fingers in the silky length. Holding her while she let out a sob.

"I thought you were dead," she whispered. "I saw the flames, and I thought..."

I kissed her throat. "It'd take more than a little explosion to kill us. We're badasses. Just like you." We were, but on this occasion we'd been more lucky than badass.

If the explosion went off when we were inside the cottage, we would have been blown to pieces. Not even the most kick-ass person would have survived that.

"I don't feel like a badass," she said. "I killed people today. I feel... numb."

"I'd be worried if you weren't numb," I said. "When that wears off, you'll need our support."

She might come apart for a while, but she'd be fine. We'd see to that. "If you felt nothing, or if you enjoyed it, I'd be worried."

"Frost enjoys it," she pointed out. "So does my brother."

"They're both fucked in the head," I said lightly. "But it's part of their charm. We wouldn't have them any other way, would we?"

She sniffed. "No, we wouldn't. I just thought..."

I drew my head back to look in her eyes. "What did you think?" I asked gently.

"I thought... I thought I might enjoy it too." Her eyes shone with unshed tears.

"You were worried you'd like killing?" I guessed. "You thought you might be fucked in the head too?"

She pressed her lips together and nodded. "I think that's what everyone expected of me. I'm supposed to be like my brother. But I'm not. I don't want to kill everyone in sight."

I smiled slightly. "That's good, because I'm in your direct line of sight."

She batted my shoulder. "I definitely don't want

to kill you, or any of my guys. I meant... other people." She blinked and looked at me like she wasn't seeing me, she was lost in thought.

"Except Dominic King and Otis Skinner. They were in on this. All of this. So was Nyla." She briefly explained what the other woman's role was in everything that happened over the last few months.

"I'm not sure I shouldn't kill her," I said dryly.

"I think we can work with her," Chelsea said. "If we can't, then we'll have to deal with her." She spoke like a true mafia princess, like she'd finally stepped into that role.

What did I think about that? I wasn't sure. To me, she'd always be hot as hell, no matter who or what she was, but I didn't want her to lose her soul in the process.

"First, we need to get you out of here," I said. "Then we deal with King and Skinner."

"We're in," Hunter said. He and Parker stood at the bottom of the steps, on the runway. "Reuben will want us to take care of them anyway. We might as well be proactive and volunteer."

Parker sighed. "Maybe then he'll give us a break to spend with the girls."

"He better," Hunter said. "Otherwise, I quit."

"I vote you tell him that," Parker said. "I'm not going to."

"I'll make sure he gives you a break," Mina told them both. As the mother of a five-year-old boy and a three-year-old girl, she'd know what it was like to be a new parent. Daze too, although her daughter was closer to ten years old now.

"We're not dealing with anyone until everyone gets a good night's rest," Ice said firmly. He quickly recovered from the disappointment of missing out on torturing Jones, and was instead hovering near Chelsea, looking a combination of relieved and worried.

I'd never seen siblings, apart from the Brantley twins, as close as Chelsea and Ice. When he suggested we actually stand in front of the plane I thought he'd lost his mind completely. But he was serious and we'd all followed him. Not one of us would have been able to live with ourselves if that plane took off, taking her with it. It was the most intense game of chicken I'd ever played in my life, and I never wanted to do it again.

In a fight between an aircraft and humans, the chances were we would have lost.

Yet, none of us flinched. We'd just stood there, side by side, ready to see if that windscreen was bullet-proof or not. Or one of the side windows. There was never really a plan. In the end, we didn't need one. Chelsea saved herself.

"I could do with some sleep," Chelsea said. "After a long soak. And some chocolate. Maybe some pizza."

"Whatever you want." I kissed her mouth, savouring the feel of her lips on mine. So warm, plump and soft. "We'll organise it."

I took her hand and walked with her down the steps onto the runway. All the rest of her guys arrayed themselves around us. Nothing and no one was getting past us again. We'd deal with King and Skinner, and finally we'd be free to get on with our lives together.

In twenty-four hours, it would be over.

I hoped.

I managed to score a seat beside Chelsea in the back of one of the SUVs. Dallas and Frost tried to get around each other to sit on her other side, but it was Jay who got there first. Mumbling, they sat behind us, squashed in with Storm. Atlas sat beside Gianni, who volunteered to drive us home.

I clicked in my seatbelt and sat staring at her until she turned to me and blinked a couple of times.

"What?" she asked.

"I'm trying to get my head around the fact you're here," I said. I brushed hair off her face with the back of my knuckles.

"That might be the longest sentence I ever heard you say," she teased lightly.

"You have that effect on me." I cupped her cheek and ran my thumb over her smooth skin and down to her jaw line. "I might become a chatterbox."

She laughed softly. "I can't see that happening. But you can tell me how you all got to the airfield. Seeing you drive up like that, it was like something out of a movie. Except without a rocket launcher."

"I'll remember to bring one next time," I said. I told her everything that happened since she left the cottage, using as few words as I could.

"I've never seen your brother look so angry. Jones is lucky he's dead. He would have lived a long time down in Ice's workroom. A long, painful time." I stopped for a beat before asking, "How long does it take before he gets bored with someone?"

"I think we would have found out," she said.

I had no regrets about Carlos Jones' death, even if it denied her brother some fun. I was happy that part of all of this was over. Thanks to Nyla Fox. If it wasn't for her, things would have turned out differently.

I shifted in my seat, restless after so long with little activity. "Being chained up in one place would be my worst nightmare. Even if your brother didn't lay a hand on me."

"Is that why you work out so much?" she asked gently. "Because you can't keep still?"

I glanced around to see the guys all looking out the window, not listening to our whispered conversation. I swallowed and turned back to Chelsea.

"I work out a lot because I never liked what I saw in the mirror. I always felt like I was... bigger than I should be. When I was a kid, I was, and it stuck with me. No matter how much I worked out, it never felt like enough."

I looked down to my knees. "Then it got to be a habit and an obsession. Now, if I don't do it I might go crazy."

"You know your perception isn't accurate, right?" she asked. "Your body is incredible. I know I've told you tons of times not to overdo it. If you do, you could give yourself a permanent injury." She sounded every bit the doctor, but the concerned girl-friend at the same time.

"Is this where you tell me I need therapy?" I asked.

"Do you think you need it?" She placed a hand on my knee.

I didn't want to answer that, but I finally managed a nod. "I guess I do. Before it goes too far."

"We all need help sometimes," she said. "Even big, badass mafia dudes like you. Even badass rugby dudes. It's nothing to be ashamed of. In fact, I could use some professional help myself, especially after last night. And today. Maybe we could go together?" She squeezed my knee.

"That's a good idea." I put my arm around her and pulled me to her, holding her close while we watched the landscape slide past. We'd be back in Dusk Bay in an hour or so, back to reality.

Right then, I just wanted to enjoy a quiet moment while it lasted.

Chapter Nineteen

Chelsea

"I don't know about you, but I'm exhausted." I rubbed a hand over my eyes and brushed hair off my face.

"Me too," Frost agreed. He carried my bag inside before placing it down on the floor and putting his arms around me. "I got a few minutes of sleep while Storm was driving, but I dreamt about you." He nestled his face down into my neck. "I didn't think I'd ever see you again."

I leaned against him, drawing comfort from his firm, warm body. "I didn't think I'd see any of you again either. When I saw the cottage explode..." I sniffled, not caring if tears trickled down my cheeks. No one could blame me for crying right now, not even me.

"It takes more than a little explosion to take us out," he said lightly.

I leaned back and looked up at him. "You must have been scared. You came so close to..." I sniffed again.

He brushed the pad of his thumb over my cheek, wiping away a tear. "Okay, I admit it. I was scared. A couple of metres closer and we would have been barbecue. I like a good barbecue as much as the next guy, but I don't want to be on the menu." He managed a lopsided smile.

I gave him a watery smile in response. "I don't want you to be on the menu either. Not like that."

"Oh really?" One of his eyebrows rose. "How do you want me on the menu?"

"Same question," Storm said. He came to stand beside us and put his arms around both of us. He looked even more exhausted than I felt. Neither of them, or Ramsey, got any sleep the night before. The rest of us were lucky, in an unlucky way. I hadn't slept much, but a little bit was better than nothing. After this, I might sleep for a month. Why not? I had nothing else to do.

"Why don't we start with a bite to eat and a shower?" I suggested. "We're going to need our rest.

No doubt we were going to be fielding a shit ton of questions about Carlos Jones."

Reuben Brantley was going to want to know everything in detail. My brother would handle most of it, for now at least. Until Reuben had questions he didn't know the answers to.

"I'll order something to eat," Atlas said as he and Jay stepped in from the garage.

"Not so fast," Storm said. "I, for one, want to know what the fuck you were playing at?" He stepped away from me and Frost and crossed his arms.

Atlas rubbed a hand over the back of his neck. "What is there to know? I've been working for the Brantley family for years, you know that."

"I also know you turned your back on us out at the cottage. You let that prick take Chelsea away." Storm looked ready to take aim, regardless of what Atlas said.

"I gave us all the best chance of surviving," Atlas said unapologetically. "If things went down any differently, you really would be dead right now. If you were dead, you couldn't have told Ice and the others what happened." His gaze bore into Storm, daring him to disagree.

Storm returned the look. "You seemed very chummy with Jones."

"I like being alive." Atlas shrugged. "I like all of us being alive. I think the words you're looking for are 'thank you'."

"Thank you," Frost said without reservation. He gave Storm a meaningful look.

"Atlas is right," Ramsey said. "He did what he had to do to keep us all alive." He patted Atlas on the shoulder on the way past.

"Thanks," Atlas said.

Storm eyed them all before grabbing up his bag and carrying it into his room.

"He'll come around," I said softly. "We're all just tired. Atlas, you said something about ordering food? I might have a quick shower before it arrives."

"I'll come with you," Frost and Dallas said at the same time.

Frost grinned. "Someone has to wash your back."

"Someone has to wash yours too," Jay said to him, smiling awkwardly.

"Sounds like a good plan to me." Frost took my hand and Jay's and pulled us towards my room, leaving Dallas to hurry along behind.

"Is pizza good?" Atlas called out behind us.

"Carbs sound perfect right now," Frost called back.

I glanced over my shoulder to Ramsey, who caught my eye and nodded. Normally he would have insisted on a salad, but after the conversation in the car, maybe he'd have pizza this once. The team dietician wouldn't be happy if they knew, but none of us was going to tell them. Right now, what we needed was comfort food.

The moment we stepped into my bedroom, I started shedding my clothes, tossing garments left and right, not caring where they landed. This was no sexy striptease, this was a tired effort to get naked and under the hot water as quickly as possible.

Moments later, the steam was filling the bathroom and I was surrounded by three, naked football players, each one half-erect already.

"Let me wash your hair," Frost offered. He turned me around so my back was to him and started to rub shampoo all over my scalp, massaging it in with his fingers.

"That feels so good," I said, my chin tilted so the shampoo wouldn't get in my eyes.

"You feel so good," Dallas said, rubbing body wash over my stomach and up over my breasts. He palmed my nipples before leaning in to kiss one, then the other. Shaking water off his face, he sank to his knees and pressed his face against my thighs.

I opened for him, letting him carefully wash and rinse my pussy before licking excess water away with his tongue. That turned to teasing and tasting my folds and sucking my piercing.

Jay scooted over behind Frost, washing his back like he'd said he would. While Frost washed the shampoo out of my hair, Jay cleaned his. Lucky for us this shower had multiple shower heads, so no one had to get cold, and we could all wash at once.

Jay turned Frost around and carefully washed his cock before joining Dallas on his knees. He wrapped his lips around Frost's cock. Cradling the other player's balls in his hand, he started to suck.

"The shower was a good idea," Frost moaned.

I glanced over him and responded with a throaty laugh. That was all I could do when Dallas had me so close to coming. Even after all we'd been through, even as tired as I was, he managed to get me right to the edge and over. Coming as the water washed down my body.

I barely came back to Earth when he had me pressed against the side of the shower, my leg around his waist, his cock deep inside me. He thrust in rhythm with Jay's sucks, and the roll of Frost's hips.

"I'm going to come," Frost panted.

"Me too," Dallas agreed. "So... Close."

It didn't surprise me he was already close. He always was; I loved that about him. Whatever he did, he threw all of himself into it, including this. Especially this.

"Come for me," I told them both. "Be good boys and come for me."

Both of their eyes widened, but they did as they were told, thrusting harder and faster before groaning in unison and spilling themselves before sagging, tired but satisfied.

Frost stepped away from Jay, grabbed his hand and pulled him to his feet. "I should—"

"You don't have to, if you're tired," Jay said, in spite of his thick erection.

"I'm never too tired for a blowjob," Frost said with a grin. He lowered himself to his knees without hesitation and wrapped his mouth around Jay's cock.

With one eye on them, I carefully washed Dallas' back, scrubbing with a loofah while he lowered his head and enjoyed the way it felt. I washed his shoulders, his ass and down his legs before turning him around to wash the front of him.

Not surprisingly, he was already hard again. I washed his firm chest and down to his chiselled abs before moving down to his thighs, carefully avoiding touching his cock.

"Chelsea..." He groaned softly.

I grinned at him before putting the loofah back and wrapping my fingers around his erection. His skin was so smooth and hot and hard. Blood pumped through him, making him throb. He rocked his hips a couple of times, his eyes rolling back in his head.

I went on stroking him as I knelt in front of him and took him all the way into my mouth, to the back of my throat.

He groaned, long and low before he started to thrust slowly, with more restraint than usual. Careful and deliberate, wanting to enjoy every moment.

I cupped his balls, stroking them, spoiling them like they deserved to be spoiled. After all, they worked hard. Energetic balls like these needed extra attention.

I slipped my mouth off his cock to tease his balls with my tongue and suck on them gently.

"Fuck... Chelsea." He wrapped his fingers around a fistful of my hand and groaned.

I looked up at him and smiled before moving my mouth back to his cock, sucking him deeply, tasting every drop of pre-cum that soon became cum as he exploded. A wash of sweet, salty goodness filling my mouth. He went on thrusting into me even after I swallowed, still slow and deliberate before reluctantly sliding out of me.

I glanced over just as Jay came inside Frost's mouth, grunting and grinding against him, his eyes half closed as he enjoyed his orgasm.

Frost's eyes met mine as he pulled his mouth of Jay and swallowed. "So fucking tasty." He licked his lips and grinned. "If I could bottle that, I'd be rich."

I didn't bother to point out he was already rich. I just let Dallas pull me to my feet while Frost got to his.

"We should get dry," Jay said, leaning in to kiss him quickly. "We're all tired and the pizza is probably here by now." He looked like he needed a few moments to himself, so none of us stopped him when he stepped out of the shower and grabbed a towel before hurrying out.

"I could eat more." Frost turned off the water and gestured for Dallas and I to step out ahead of him.

Chapter Twenty

Chelsea

A week of sleep would have been nice, but a night was all we got. One in which we all crashed down hard, barely moving until later in the morning. We finally managed to drag ourselves up and have breakfast before my brother turned up at the door. Smiling, like always.

"You boys won't mind if I have a few minutes alone with my sister," he said, shooing them out.

"What if we do mind?" Storm asked.

"Do we?" Frost asked him.

Storm shrugged. "I guess not. Don't take long." He narrowed his eyes at Ice, as though my brother would be intimidated.

Ice just grinned and led me over to the couch, sitting me down before lowering himself beside me.

"How are you this morning?" he asked carefully.

I leaned back and sighed. "Conflicted. Glad to be home. Relieved Carlos Jones is dead. Those are some ripples which are going to be felt for a while."

"They will." He placed his hands behind his head and crossed his legs at his knees. "But I want to know how *you* are doing. You're more important to me than the upheaval in the Crimson Vipers. You're the one who killed him."

Yes," I said in a small voice. "He was going to kill Nyla. Everyone else was frozen, like they forgot how to move or something." I shook my head slowly. "It all happened so fast."

"You killed two more of his men on that plane," he stated.

"Are you my therapist now?" I teased half-heartedly.

He lowered his hands, placing his arms on his thighs and leaning towards me. "If you need one. I know you, you'll be dwelling on what happened. Beating yourself up about it, although none of it was your fault. So, talk to me."

I pressed my lips together for a moment. "I killed three men yesterday. Three more than I've ever killed before."

"And you feel... How?" He raised his eyebrows at me in question.

"I don't know," I admitted. "I'm not sure if I feel anything yet. Is that normal?"

He smiled. "You're asking me about normal? I should refer you to Ares, he'll tell you. For the record, I think it's perfectly normal. But something else is bothering you. Out with it."

"I never could get anything past you, could I?" I asked.

"Never," he agreed. "That's what big brothers are for. Go on, you can talk to me. What's going through your mind?"

"I'm worried about what happens after," I said slowly. "What happens when I'm not numb anymore?"

"Do you have the overwhelming urge to chain someone to the ceiling and peel off layers of skin with a vegetable peeler?" he asked.

I grimaced. "No."

"Do you want to pull off fingernails with a set of pliers?" he asked.

"Also no," I said.

"Okay, what about walking up to some stranger and slicing open their throat, feeling their warm, sticky blood coating your hand?" He opened and closed his fingers as though imagining just that.

"I don't want to do any of those things," I said.

"Then you're probably normal," he concluded. "Killing people hasn't turned you into an unhinged psychopath. Or even a hinged one."

"Is that what you are?" I teased.

He smiled. "Something like that. Except that I have empathy, which the average psychopath doesn't."

"Yes, you do," I said. He wouldn't be capable of caring about me, or his partners if he didn't. But he cared about me and them, deeply.

"Is that what's had you worried all these years?" he asked. "You thought you might end up like me?"

"I guess so," I said. "I mean, yes. No offence."

"First of all, I'd never take offence at anything you say." He counted the points off on his fingers. "Second of all, there's only room for one of me in our immediate family. Any of your boyfriends is welcome to take part, but not another Miller. Third of all, that was never going to be you. I could have told you that wasn't in your blood. Your compassion wouldn't let you do the things I do. Don't tell anyone, but you're a much nicer person than I am."

"I don't know about that," I said, "but you're right.

I never wanted to do the things you do. I was just scared to be myself in case I was wrong. Terrified, if I'm honest."

"And now?" he asked.

"Now I want to be the me I was always supposed to be," I said. "I can't fight it anymore. I don't want to."

"Is this because the Smashers fired you?" he asked gently. "Are you feeling lost?"

I considered his question carefully. "I suppose I'm feeling a little bit lost, but at the same time I'm feeling... I don't know, found? I don't know if what I thought I wanted my whole life is what I really want after all. I thought medicine was everything, but now... it might have been a side quest on the way to whatever's next."

"What is that?" he asked. "I don't think you're going to come and work with me."

"Not directly," I agreed. "I'm not sure the Brantley family is going to give me much choice in what I do. I suppose I'll have to wait and see what they want from me."

"I have a feeling that will be a lot," he said. "Starting with something in particular.

"Do I want to know?" I said with a wince. Judging by the expression on his face it didn't matter, I didn't have a choice.

Chapter Twenty One

Chelsea

I DIDN'T KNOW WHO PAID THE SECURITY GUARD to let me in without question, but she did. She smiled and nodded, waving me past. Not without an edge of urgency. She was paid to let me through, not to lose her job.

I made a mental note to check back later and make sure she didn't. If she did, I'd find her one somewhere else. One that paid so well she didn't need to take bribes.

Either way, I stepped past her and in through the side entrance.

A few people noticed me. Some stopped to stare, to ogle, but no one tried to stop me.

At some point in my life, I'd perfected the art of

pretending I belonged. I did it so well, people believed I did more often than not.

I employed that now. I also wore my official lanyard and identification around my neck. For all they knew, I'd been rehired.

One of the good things about Dusk Bay was that people didn't ask too many questions. Not about things like this. In particular, they didn't ask me. Good, because today I wouldn't have given them any answers. I was here for only one reason, and it wasn't for a social call.

Heart in my throat, I headed to the bank of elevators and took the first one heading down to the pool area.

The guys were scattered around the building, ready if I needed anything. I took their word for it that what happened to Jones had been completely suppressed. If it hadn't, I was walking into a trap.

I reminded myself the guys and my brother were listening via the microphone hidden in my bra. If anything even *looked* like going south, they'd be right there.

If they could get to me in time. This whole operation was risky, but like my brother said, I had no choice. The Brantley family wouldn't let me walk away now. Honestly, I would let myself walk away. I needed to see this all the way through to the end. In an hour or two, this would be over, one way or the other.

The elevator pinged and the doors slid open. I shoved away the thought that maybe I was walking to my execution, and stepped out, chin raised.

As planned, I pushed through the doors into the pool area as Skinner was finishing a session with one of the players. Not one of mine, so he barely gave me a glance before he hurried off to shower. The glance he did give me came with a smirk. Of course he'd read the headline or someone told him. Whatever, I wasn't letting that small detail get to me. In the scheme of things, it was barely a blip on the radar.

Skinner, on the other hand, narrowed his eyes at me. "You shouldn't be here." He was always so kind and welcoming. Not. If he was surprised to see me, he didn't show it. What did that mean? Did he know Jones was dead, or was he not privy to the cartel leader's plans? I guessed it was the latter. He was a lackey. Jones owed him no explanations. The same way Reuben Brantley owed me none.

"Hello, it's nice to see you too," I said with venomous sweetness.

He grunted, irritated at being called out,

however subtly. "Did you want something, *Miss* Miller?"

"*Doctor* Miller," I corrected. The next person who called me miss, in a derisive way, was going to feel my heel on their balls.

He clearly did it to get a response from me. The fact he had amused him. I saw that in his eyes and the faint, smug smile on his mouth.

Fucker.

"I'd question the accuracy of that, but whatever you want to believe." He shrugged. "I asked you a question. Did you want something?"

"You could say that," I said. "I'm curious what you have to gain in working for Carlos Jones."

His flinch was subtle, but it was there. He really hadn't known about Jones' plans, because he wasn't a good enough actor to hide his surprise.

"I have no idea who that is," he said trying to regain his composure. "I work for the Smashers. If that's all you've come to say, you can leave or I'll have security remove you."

"You're a crappy liar," I told him. To be honest, it felt good to be so blunt with the man. I'd walked on eggshells around him for long enough. It was time for him to bear the brunt of my real thoughts about him. Fuck with me and I'll fuck back.

"We both know you know who Jones is. But in case you need a reminder, he's the head of the Crimson Vipers. They're a cartel with connections to organised crime. Tight connections. They traffic drugs, guns, money. People. Carlos Jones thought it was a good idea to try to take on those he worked for. He got too big for his boots. Sound familiar?" I cocked my head at him and waited for an answer. Watched while he squirmed.

"What if it does?" Skinner asked. He stood beside the pool with a clipboard in his hand, held as though he might try to use it as a weapon. "I know exactly who you are, and what your connections are. You're involved as deep as he is."

"Firstly, no I'm not," I said evenly. "Secondly, I never was." Not yet anyway. My involvement was a drop in the ocean compared to Jones. "Thirdly, *was.*"

Skinner frowned. "Was what?" He clearly had no idea what I was referring to.

Good, they kept it suppressed as I'd hoped.

As if I was becoming bored with the conversation, I looked down at my nails. I really did need to make an appointment to have them done. Maybe change the colour. A nice pink next time.

"Carlos Jones was involved in a variety of things, as you know," I said. "He's now dead." I glanced up to watch that sink in. "He was killed yesterday morning."

Skinner frowned. "Bullshit. I was contacted by him an hour ago."

"Him, or the head of the Crimson Vipers?" I asked. "Because they're under new management right now. I understand they're undergoing quite the overhaul. What did they want you to do?"

"They—" he started before catching himself. "How do I know anything you're telling me is true? You could be in here stirring up trouble because you're bitter about being fired. Did you think people wouldn't find out you were a whore? It looks to me like you were putting out for the wrong people. I'm sure Dominic would have kept you on if you offered to suck him off."

He looked very pleased with himself for figuring out what he assumed was the actual reason for my visit. He was so far out I almost laughed in his face.

I snorted. "Are you about to suggest I offer you a blowjob in return for putting in a good word for me, so I can get my job back?" I made sure to inject as much sarcasm into my words as possible. I didn't want him to think I was actually offering.

"I wouldn't put it past someone like you," he said derisively.

"What do you mean 'someone like me?'" I asked. "A woman? Of course that's what you mean. Men like you always assume there's only one way for a woman to get ahead in life. With her body. You can't fathom the idea that I was at the top of my class by using my brains."

He rolled his eyes, clearly believing exactly what I accused him of. No wonder he and Jones got along.

"Tell me something, what did Jones offer you?" I asked. "Access to as many women as you could want? With or without their consent?"

He twitched. "Don't be ridiculous. That would be... illegal."

I barked a laugh. "Now you care about things being legal. You didn't flinch when Max Stanley was murdered. Or Bruce Fergus. I'm sure you won't lose any sleep over Carlos Jones either." I took a couple of steps closer. "What did he offer you?"

He backed up a step. "Power. Money." After a moment, and with some reluctance, he added, "Women."

I nodded slowly as though absorbing all of this. As if I didn't already understand everything.

"Where did those women come from?" I asked.

"I don't know." He wouldn't meet my gaze now.

"He held parties. I put in my order and he delivered. Petite, blonde. Long hair. Always long hair."

"I'm relieved to know I'm not your type," I said dryly.

My stomach turned at the very idea that he could put in a request for a particular type of woman, as though he was ordering a pizza with all the right toppings. And Jones would send his people out to find them if they didn't already have them in stock. I wasn't naïve enough to think it didn't happen, especially with powerful men around the world, but hearing about it directly? That was another thing entirely.

"I prefer a woman who knows her place," he said, now looking at me like he was repulsed in some way.

I won't lie, the feeling was completely mutual. Correction, repulsive wasn't a strong enough word to describe him and the people he associated with. Evil might fit better.

"Did King take part in these parties? Who else was there? If you give me some names, I'll make sure my connections go easy on you. After all, you've proven to be resourceful. You might be useful to the people I work with."

He saw the bait and took it like a lifeline. "King was very much present. He has a preference for women who look like you. Dark hair and an attitude. He liked to remind them he was in charge."

I fucking bet he did. If he wasn't already on my shit list, he was now. There was a world of difference between being dominant in the bedroom, and in a relationship, and being dominant without consent. I didn't need Skinner to paint me a picture. The one in my mind was bad enough.

"Who else was present?" I might as well try to catch as many fish as I could.

"Carlos Jones," Skinner said. He rattled off a bunch of other names, most of which I recognised from around Dusk Bay and around the country. Several politicians, a couple of businessmen, some high profile actors. Some I was surprised by, others not.

I nodded when he finished the list and leaned forward to speak into my microphone, to make it clear everything we said was overheard.

"Did you get all of that?" I asked.

"Every word," my brother said in the earphone in my ear.

Skinner stared at me for a moment in horror. "You fucking bitch!" He threw the clipboard aside and lunged at me, sending us both flying into the pool.

Chapter Twenty Two

Chelsea

I HIT THE WATER WITH A SPLASH.

Skinner landed beside me. He reached for me. Grabbed me by the front of my shirt and pulled me toward him.

I kicked out at him, one shoe connecting with his knee before falling off my foot. I made a grab for his hands and dug my nails into his skin. They slipped and slid before scraping hard enough for him to grunt in pain.

He loosened his grip and went for my throat instead. Wrapped his large, wet hands around my neck. Squeezed.

I kicked at him with the other foot. Kicking and kicking and digging my nails in deeper.

I was already starting to feel lightheaded. If I

didn't get a breath soon, I'd drown before he strangled me.

I kicked with everything I had. Let go of him and
pushed through the water, trying to get to the
surface. I managed to stick my face out and suck in a
breath of precious air before he dragged me back
under again.

I curled my fingers around his and tried to pull
them off my throat. They wouldn't budge. They
were tight around my neck like he was fused there.
Like a collar with no hinge.

Fuck.

Don't panic, I told myself. *The minute you panic,
you're dead. If you die, they win.*

Fuck that.

I gave up trying to dislodge him and wrapped my
own around his neck instead. My teeth clenched, I
heaved and rolled us over so he was below me, under
the water. Every so often, I was able to find the
surface and gasp for air. It wasn't enough. The pressure on my throat was too great.

My vision was starting to turn black.

He can't win.

With everything I had, I pulled him sideways,
trying to ram his hand into the side of the pool. The
water slowed the momentum, making the slam a

little more than a tap. He barely would have felt it, certainly not enough to knock him loose.

Oh great, I was going to die here. I'd already had a bad enough week as it was. Did it really have to end this way? To say it sucked was an understatement. After everything I'd gone through with my guys, it was bullshit.

Yes, we considered the possibility things might go this way before I confronted him here. I mean, bad guy, water. We'd be crazy if we didn't consider it. At some point, we'd all thought about doing the same to him. This was probably his idea of a wet dream. So to speak.

We'd planned for this, though. A couple of the guys were supposed to be close. Close enough they could pull me out quickly if I went in.

Not close enough, apparently. No, I was going to drown. They wouldn't reach me in time. They were going to be devastated. Hell, I was devastated. The fact they were going to rip Skinner apart was no consolation for dying like this. Nothing would be. This was a million kinds of fucked up. I took some solace in knowing they'd bring down King and the whole network of exploitation and violation of women. At least my death wouldn't be for nothing.

The guys might not see it that way for a while though. They were going to—

Skinner's grip went slack before dropping away from me.

What the hell?

At the same time, a firm grip circled my wrist and pulled me up, all the way out of the water, to the side of the pool. Dripping and gasping, I was lowered down to the floor, where I collapsed in a heap. I didn't know how long I lay on the pebbled tiles, gasping for breath, trying to clear my head. As far as I would could tell, I wasn't dead. Unless the other side looked a lot like being alive. Judging by the way my lungs hurt, I was very much not dead.

"Chelsea?"

That was Ramsey's voice.

I coughed a couple of times. "I'm okay," I managed to say. My voice was strained, but I could form those words. "I'm okay."

"Thank fuck." He breathed out a heavy sigh of relief. "I didn't think I got to you in time."

I blinked and looked up to where he crouched beside me. "You did." He was a beautiful sight to see right now. Always, but especially right now. "I never had any doubt."

I decided not to dwell the last few thoughts I had before he pulled me out of the water. Of course they never would have let me die. Not if they could help it.

I slid my gaze over to the pool. Skinner lay face down, blood trickling from his head, mingling with the pool water.

It was then I realised Dallas was standing beside the pool, a football boot in his hands. I could make out the spikes on the sole.

"Did he..." I asked softly.

"Hit Skinner on the head with a footy boot? Yes, he did," Ramsey said proudly. "He didn't even hesitate."

Dallas turned his face slowly to look at us. "I wasn't going to let him kill you," he whispered. The boot dropped from his hands and he knelt down beside me to gather me up, not caring that I was drenched.

"We heard what he did," Ramsey said. "He deserved it."

"Yeah, he did," I agreed. "We need to get to King before he finds out about this."

Ramsey made a sound of agreement in the back of his throat. "The camera is off, but we need to deal with this before someone walks in."

He stood and gestured to Dallas to help him. They each took hold of an ankle and a wrist and hauled a dripping Skinner up out of the water, over to the side of the pool. "We'll put him in the change room. With any luck, he won't be found in there for a while."

They hefted him and carried him away, easing open the change room door before taking him through and out of sight.

I took a few moments to regain my composure before placing my palms on the tiles and pushing myself to my feet. Both of my shoes were floating on the water, probably ruined.

My jeans, T-shirt and Smashers hoodie were drenched through. I was cold, but rather than being angry, scared or even traumatised, I had an idea. Was it too out there? Possibly, but I needed to try. Jones hadn't broken me. Skinner hadn't killed me. I could do this. For all of those women, I'd do this.

I grabbed a towel from the basket near the door and wrapped it around my shoulders. I was just pulling it closed over my chest when the guys hurried out of the change room.

"We need to find you some dry clothes," Ramsey said, looking worried.

"Not yet." I told him what I had in mind.

Neither of them seemed to like the idea, but they both sighed and conceded it might just work.

Chapter Twenty Three

Ramsey

I STAYED CLOSE BESIDE CHELSEA THE WHOLE way to the elevators and during the ride. I didn't have to pretend to play the part of dutiful boyfriend all the way to the executive offices. It wasn't an act. Neither Dallas nor I would let her far enough away from us that we couldn't touch her by just raising a hand slightly.

"Are you sure about this?" Dallas asked as we approached King's office.

More and more people stopped to look at us as we walked past. Some curious, most looking at Chelsea with concern. Damp hair framed her pale face, making her look vulnerable. Innocent even. If I didn't know her better, I might be fooled too.

"I'm sure," she said. "We can do this."

We took her hands and walked straight past King's personal assistant who sat at her desk. She rose, put out a hand to stop us, but we ignored her.

I didn't even spare her a glance, but I remained on alert in case she tried anything.

We walked into King's office and closed the door behind us.

He sat behind his desk, eyes on his computer until he finally looked up at us. A range of emotions crossed his features. Irritation. Surprise. Confusion. Then concern. Not entirely sincere, but concern nonetheless.

He rose to his feet and placed his palms on the desk, to either side of his laptop. "What happened?" he asked, directing the question to Chelsea. "I assume there's a reason you're dripping on my carpet?"

She sniffed. "I'm sorry." Her voice wavered like she was about to burst into tears. She looked as though she was. Her reddened eyes glistened.

I knew it wasn't entirely fake. Skinner tried to kill her. That would rattle anyone. It sure as hell rattled me. If we'd taken a couple of moments longer, she would have drowned, or he would have strangled her. We would have lost her. I would have lost her.

That reality sank in with her, maybe before I

pulled her from the water, leaving her shaken. I wanted to take her away from this building, wrap her up in a warm blanket and tuck her away from the world.

When this was over, I might do exactly that.

"You have nothing to be sorry about," I told her gently. "Just tell him what happened."

She swallowed hard and nodded. "Okay."

"Tell me what?" King pushed himself back from his desk and walked around it. He stopped in front of us, eyes on Chelsea.

I remembered what Skinner said about King ordering women who look like her. I'd be blind to miss the hint of lust in his gaze. A part of him was enjoying her vulnerability. If Dallas and I weren't here, he'd probably act on it. For him, this was some kind of fantasy scenario.

Sick fucker.

"I went down to the pool to speak to Doctor Skinner," Chelsea said, her voice still shaky. "I was hoping he'd keep training me in aqua therapy. Even though I don't work here anymore, I still want to learn. Maybe I could, I don't know, start my own therapy business. Or... or something." She shook her head and blinked until tears rolled down her damp cheeks.

"I'm sure you'd do very well at that," King said

soothingly. "I understand why you'd like to train more with Otis. He's very good at what he does."

He was very good at being a complete and utter asshole, I agreed silently. The world was better off without him.

"Yeah." Chelsea sniffed. "But when I went down there, I found him lying in the pool. I jumped into trying to save him. But it was—" She let out a very convincing sob. "It was too late. I tried to resuscitating him. The guys did too." She looked from Dallas to me, then back to King before whispering, "He's dead."

Surprise was back on King's face, but it was short lived. He nodded slowly. "That's unfortunate. I'm not sure I believe that's what happened though, Doctor Miller."

She cocked her head at him and sniffed. "I don't understand. What are you saying?"

He crossed his arms. "I'm suggesting maybe it wasn't an accident."

She sighed and stood up straighter, the façade gone.

"Okay, you're right. I went down there to talk to him and he tried to kill me. If it wasn't for these two, I never would have survived. He tried to drown me."

"That's more like it," King said. "Why would he do a thing like that?"

"Because I gave him some bad news," she said evenly. Her voice was clear and confident now. I made a note not to play poker with her. I'd lose my shirt and a whole lot more. Although, I'd willingly give her my shirt and everything else I had. "I told him Carlos Jones is dead."

Once again, King schooled surprise off his face. "How would you know a thing like that?"

"You mean, how do I know when you don't?" she asked.

She actually seemed amused by his question. This woman. If anyone doubted she was a mafia princess before this, they wouldn't now. She stepped into the role like she'd done it all her life. Whatever happened from here on out, she was never looking back.

"Because I killed him."

King pressed his finger to his lower lip. "You're an interesting woman, Doctor Miller. You killed Carlos Jones, then you killed Otis Skinner."

"Oh, I didn't kill Skinner," she said lightly. "That was Dallas. Right in the nick of time too. Word of advice, don't let him hit you with a football boot."

"I wasn't planning to let him do such a thing,"

King said. "Have you come to kill me too?" For the first time, he looked slightly nervous. He measured us and seemed to be reminding himself at least two of us were big, strong rugby players. And Chelsea, she knew how to kill a man and not leave a mark. Anyone who underestimated her was a fool.

"I don't want to kill you," Chelsea said easily.

"You don't?" he asked carefully. He knew something was going on, but couldn't figure out what it was. Maybe she'd offer him some kind of deal in return for his cooperation. He could become one of the Brantley family lackeys, or something like that.

"No, I don't," she agreed.

"But I do." I pulled a small knife out of my pocket, flicked open the blade and drove it straight into King's chest, right through his heart.

His eyes bulged, mouth dropped open. He lowered his arms to his sides before starting to fall forward. All three of us grabbed him and lowered him the rest of the way down to the floor.

"Now who's dripping on the carpet?" Chelsea asked. Blood was trickling from King's chest, pumping a couple of times before his heart stopped completely.

"That would be him," Frost said as he opened the

door and stepped in behind us. He seemed slightly disappointed to get here after we killed King. No doubt he'd had fantasies of his own about doing exactly that. Honestly, I would have waited for him, but I was done with King and his bullshit. And the way he was looking at Chelsea like somehow she might still factor in his future plans, even if he was a lackey.

"He's not looking too well." Storm followed Frost in, his eyes on King.

"I don't know, he looks fine to me," Atlas said as he ushered Jay in with him. "Just right." He patted me on the shoulder.

I managed a small smile. "He got what he deserved. That's all."

"Yeah, he did," Storm agreed. He wrapped his arms around Chelsea and held her close. "It looks like we going to need a new GM. Again. I vote we get a better one this time."

"Coach can come back now." Frost looked excited. Apparently he had already recovered from his disappointment at not being the one to kill King. Frost was resilient if nothing else. We all were. What choice did we have, living this lifestyle? And they thought playing football was tough.

"After we get this mess cleaned up," I said. I

pulled out my phone and sent off a text. "They shouldn't be long. Let's get Chelsea home."

I gave King a last look before herding everyone out. King's assistant was gone when we walked past her desk. By the look of it, she'd cleared out and bolted. Under the circumstances, that was a wise move. If I was her, I'd be long gone. Along with anyone else who worked for Jones.

Finally, we could reclaim our team and get back to living our lives. With our perfect, beautiful mafia princess. I silently corrected myself. She'd gone from being a reluctant princess to a queen. Our queen.

"Home sounds good," I said. "I could use a workout. "I grinned when Chelsea looked back at me, a frown on her brow. "Not overdoing it. I promise." I intended to keep that promise and many more. Including going to therapy. We'd faced down a lot of demons in the last few weeks, I could deal with this one. After all, I had my family to support me and help me through.

What more could a guy want?

Chapter Twenty Four

"I'S LONG PAST TIME WE CHRISTENED THIS space," I said as we filed down the stairs to the basement.

"Funny, I was thinking the same thing," Frost said.

We'd left the stadium right before the story of Max Stanley's return broke. At some point, the press would learn about the tragic drowning of Otis Skinner, and the mysterious demise of Dominic King. That was a problem for the future. For now, we were focused on being together and mending any of the bridges that got damaged in the last while.

For the most part, we got out unscathed. Although, I might not go in a swimming pool again for a while.

"We've been busy," Ramsey remarked. He seemed more relaxed than I'd seen him before.

In fact, now I thought about it, all of the guys were more relaxed than they'd been. So was I. Relaxed and looking forward to getting on with my life.

"Where do we start?" Frost looked around at all the toys and apparatuses in the basement.

Storm let out a laugh. When we all turned to him questioningly, he pointed. "An industrial size bottle of lubricant with a pump. I like it. You really did think of everything." He put an arm around Frost and loudly kissed his cheek.

"To be honest, that was the first thing on my list," Frost said, blushing slightly. "I figured we'd need it."

"You figured right." Atlas placed his hands on Jay's shoulders and steered him over to the sex couch.

Before anyone else could move, Dallas grabbed my hand and tugged me over to the swing in the corner.

"I've always wanted to try one of these," he said.

I smiled. "You're in for a treat then." I let him help me out of my clothes and did the same to him, while the others stripped off.

Storm and Frost headed over to the side to check out the array of toys and Ramsey leaned against the wall, watching Dallas lift me onto the swing and get me comfortable.

I pressed my feet into the stirrups and leaned back while Dallas knelt in front of me. My legs were wide open, giving him easy access to my pussy with his mouth and fingers.

"So fucking beautiful," he whispered before diving in, thoroughly tasting me with his tongue and fucking me with his hand.

"She certainly is," Ramsey agreed, his eyes drinking me in, watching my breasts bounce as I rocked my hips against Dallas' mouth, making the swing move with me.

The feeling of him between my legs was as good as the view. Atlas had Jay bent over, thrusting into him slowly and carefully. Storm had Frost blindfolded and was teasing him with a vibrating wand, sliding it in and out of his rear hole.

"Fun for the whole family," Ramsey remarked.

I grinned and waved him over gesturing him closer so I could kiss him while Dallas fucked me with his mouth. I didn't want anyone to be left out. Not of this and not of anything else. We were family and families took care of each other.

He pressed his tongue between my lips and

thrust into my mouth while caressing my breasts and pinching my nipples.

All of the attention had me ready to come quicker than I would have thought was possible. These guys, they always knew what I liked and how to give it to me. Not like any other man I'd ever known. I was the luckiest girl on the face of the planet and would be for the rest of my life.

"Come for me," Ramsey said between kisses. "Come for me like a good girl."

"Who says I'm a good girl?" I asked.

"I do," he said. "But if you're going to talk back like that, I might have to punish you."

My guys, always threatening me with a good time.

"Maybe I don't want to come," I said, then moaned as Dallas stroked my G-spot just right, taking away all self-control and throwing me off like the relentless flow of a waterfall plunging down a cliff. I rocked against him harder, while Ramsey cupped the back of my head to hold me still so he could kiss me through my orgasm.

I was barely down when Ramsey pulled me off the swing and turned me around to lie back down on it, the seat supporting my stomach and the top strap supporting my chest.

"Get a paddle," Ramsey said to Dallas as he rose to his feet.

I wriggled to get more comfortable before Dallas hurried back and handed the paddle to Ramsey.

"Tell me again you're not a good girl," Ramsey said lightly running the side of the paddle over my ass cheek.

"I'm very good," I said, quivering with anticipation. "So good, but I need a reminder."

"I agree." He brought the paddle down on my ass, the leather slapping together, and making it sound harder than it was.

The delicious sting made me moan.

"Just like that."

He brought the paddle down on my cheek again a couple of times before paddling the other cheek.

"Ramsey..." Dallas sounded pained.

Ramsey paddled me one more time before tossing it aside and swinging me around, until Dallas' cock was right in front of my face.

With a groan of relief, Dallas pressed his cock between my lips.

At the same time, Ramsey parted my legs and stepped between them his hands on my hips. He positioned his cock outside my entrance and pushed himself inside me.

I felt like I was floating on air with two of my guys thrusting into me at the same time. This swing was definitely a good idea.

I glanced to the side to see Jay lying on the couch, Frost's mouth on his cock while Storm and Atlas stood behind them, Storm thrusting into Frost's ass while Atlas watched and gave them orders. Okay, gave Frost and Jay orders. Storm would never do what he told him to. They'd come a long way though. He wasn't telling Atlas to fuck off anymore. Not that I heard anyway.

"I'm going to come," Dallas whispered.

"Not until I tell you to," Ramsey said.

Dallas looked over at him and grimaced, but pressed his teeth together and fucked my mouth more slowly.

Being the good girl I was, I sucked harder, making his eyes roll back in his head.

"I can see me using the paddle a lot," Ramsey said.

I would have grinned at him, but with my mouth full, all I could do was laugh, letting my body shake so he knew I was amused. I was here for all the paddling. To give and receive.

"I can't," Dallas ground out. "I need to come."

"Not yet," Ramsey insisted.

"Do you need some help over here?" Atlas stepped over, crossed his arms and looked down at me. "I believe I heard Ramsey tell you not to come."

Dallas looked at him with a, 'not you too,' expression on his face.

"Maybe I should take your place," Atlas suggested. "That will help you wait."

"I can hold on," Dallas said, quickly, desperately.

Atlas nodded his head slowly. "Good, do as you're told. Otherwise Ramsey might use that paddle on you."

That stripped away the last of Dallas' self-control. He groaned and came hard, ejaculating a mouthful of cum down my throat so fast I gagged before swallowing it down in a hurry.

"I guess we know where he stands," Atlas said with a grin.

Dallas shot him a look before sliding his cock out of my mouth and stepping back. "I'm okay with Chelsea paddling me."

"I'm okay with that too," I said. I licked my lips, making sure I had every drop collected and swallowed. I wouldn't want to miss a single one.

A moment later, Jay cried out as he came, quickly followed by Storm, thrusting harder into Frost's before spilling himself inside.

Ramsey came next, pounding into me with even strokes, his skin slapping against mine in perfect rhythm before he grunted, stopped and lost himself deep inside me. He slumped down over me, catching his breath.

I looked around the room at my guys, all naked and with a sheen of sweat. All of them smiling, looking comfortable and satisfied. No one shooting at us. No one telling anyone else to fuck off. No one feeling the need to run and hide from anyone else.

Just six incredible guys brought together as brothers and lovers as well as being a team. Someday, they'd stop playing football together, but their bond would never break.

Long after they stopped being Smashers, they'd still be mine.

Now and forever.

Epilogue

Chelsea

"So we said to him, we'll buy the team," Hunter said, toasting us with a beer. "And he agreed. Eventually. We paid more for it than we should, but it'll be worth it."

"I don't know how I feel about you owning my team." Storm gave both twins a dubious look.

"Too late." Parker grinned. "We already do. But it's a good thing."

Storm didn't look so sure.

"The twins will do better with the team than the last management," Ice said. He seemed to have gotten over his own disappointment at not being able to kill Jones, Skinner or King. The fact they were dead must have been enough to satisfy his blood thirst. Or it might have been getting drunk with Frost and comparing notes. After killing a couple of Jones' leftover minions. Now I thought about it, it was probably the last one. Hopefully their blood thirst was satisfied now. For a while anyway.

"That wouldn't be difficult," Storm conceded. "They fired my woman, kidnapped her and tried to kill her. Anything would be an improvement." He squeezed my knee.

"Speaking of that," Hunter said. "We've chosen a new GM and we've decided their first act will be to offer Chelsea back her job. Doctor Stuart is resigning soon and we want someone we can trust to take his place." He looked over to me and grinned.

"Thank you," I said sincerely. "But Divina is selling Flirts. I was thinking of buying the place and running it myself." I quickly added, "I won't be working on the stage or in any of the private rooms. I'll strictly be the boss."

I leaned my head against Storm's shoulder. "I want to make a safe space for women to work and for men to live out their fantasies. They shouldn't have to kidnap anyone to do that. Not when I can supply girls willing to work with them. If they want a petite blonde, they don't need to snatch one off the streets. I can find them one and make sure they're well paid, comfortable and safe."

"You're not going to get up and dance again?" Dallas asked.

I smiled. "Only for my boyfriends. Not when anyone else is around."

"I'm glad you said that," Parker said. "Because Lila would probably poke our eyeballs out if we saw you naked."

"I'd poke your eyes out," Storm growled. "Both of you." He glared at them like he might do just that, but they laughed. It would take more than a threat from him to intimidate either of them.

"No one is poking anyone's eyes out," I said. "There's only six men I'll ever dance for again."

"Shame," Ice said. "You were quite good." He sipped his beer, apparently unconcerned at the nine pairs of eyes who turned to stare at him. He swallowed and smiled, amused at getting a reaction out of us.

Hunter cleared his throat. "Anyway, the offer to come back as team doctor stands. We've already released a press statement to say the team was fully aware of your past employment and supported you completely. If anyone has a problem with that, they can fuck off. There's nothing wrong with women expressing their sexuality. Right, Park?"

"Right," Parker agreed. "There should be more of

it." He swallowed his last mouthful of beer. "We should get back to the babies. I miss them already."

He and Hunter made their goodbyes and hurried out the door, followed by my brother.

"You know, they're right," Storm said. "There should be more expressions of female sexuality and badassness everywhere. Which reminds me, Chelsea you never did say how you lost your virginity."

"No, I didn't." I picked up my glass of wine and took a sip.

Thank you for reading! I hope you loved Ruck Boys as much as I loved writing about them. If you're curious about how Chelsea lost her virginity, click here for a *very* taboo bonus scene.

About the Author

Maggie Alabaster was born in Canberra, but lives on the south coast of NSW Australia with her family, and a growing collection of books and anything shaped like an eggplant. She writes reverse harem with humour and a touch of darkness. And lots of peens. Sometimes her characters listen to her, but usually they run amok and she records their antics. It's a wild ride, but she loves every minute of it.

Shop direct from Maggie! Store
Sign up for Maggie's newsletter! Sign Up!
Join Maggie's reader group! Join here!
Follow Maggie on Bookbub! Click here to follow me!
Check out Maggie's website- www.maggieal abaster.com

Also by Maggie Alabaster

Entitled Sins

Good Girls Beg

MM Romantasy

Shadow and Steel

Drop-Dead Lethal

Dead Cute

Bloody Sweet

Pretty Psychos

Best Served Cold

Heart Stopping

Heart Rending

Heart Breaking

Heart Beating

Aurora Hollow duet

Take Me Slowly Part 1

Take Me Slowly Part 2

Ruck Boys

Filthy Ruck

Hard Ruck

Twisted Ruck

Bad Ruck

Dirty Ruck

Deadly Ruck

Sparrow and the Mafia Kings

Possessive

Ruined

Corrupted

Pucking Dark Hearts

Pucking Hearts Collide

Pucking Forbidden Hearts

Pucking Hardened Hearts

Dusk Bay Demons

Puck Drop

Breakaway

Power Play

Brutal Academy

Book 1 Heartless

Book 2 Cruel

Book 3 Vengeful

Court of Blood and Binding

Book 1 Song of Scent and Magic

Book 2 Crown of Mist and Heat

Book 3 Sword of Balm and Shadow

Book 4 Whisper of Frost and Flame

Dark Masque

Book 1 Bait

Book 2 Prey

Book 3 Trap

Novella A Very Dark Masque Christmas

Saving Abbie

Book 1 Pitch

Book 2 Pound

Book 3 Session

Book 4 Muse

Book 5 Rhythm

Book 6 Encore

Novella Venomous

Saving Abbie books 1-4

Saving Abbie books 4-6 + Venomous

Ruthless Claws

Book 1 Ivory

Book 2 Crimson

Book 3 Elodie

Harmony's Magic

Book 1 Summoned by Fire

Book 2 Summoned by Fate

Book 3 Summoned by Desire

Shifter's Vault

Book 1 Discarded

Book 2 Deceived

Book 3 Disgraced

My Alien Mates

Book 1 Star Warriors

Book 2 Star Defenders

Book 3 Star Protectors

Academy of Modern Magic

Book 1 Digital Magic

Book 2 Virtual Magic

Book 3 Logical Magic

Complete Collection

Summer's Harem

Book 1: Shimmer

Book 2: Glimmer

Book 3: Flicker

Complete collection

Short reads

Taken by the Snowmen

Jingle All the Way

Also by Maggie Alabaster and Erin Yoshikawa

Caught by the Tide

Book 1–Pursued by Shadows

Book 2 Pursued by Darkness

Book 3 Pursued by Monsters